My Facebook

Inamorato

Prisca D. Kagirwa

Dedication

I dedicate this book to myself, with pride in the journey that turned a lifelong dream into reality.

Acknowledgments

I would like to thank God, my family, and friends for supporting my talent and encouraging me throughout the process of publishing this book. I would like to mention a few names: my mother (Imelda Kagirwa), my sister (Kemi Kagirwa), my sister-in-law (Neema Kiondo), my friend (Sajda Salehe), my brother (Lambert Tibaigana), and my sister (Suzan Damas).

I also want to express my gratitude for the support and strong partnership in creating this book with the Ashbery publishing company.

About The Author

Prisca Kagiwa is a woman, a mother, a sister, and the youngest daughter of the wonderful Mr. and Mrs. Kagirwa. Born and raised in Dar es Salaam, Tanzania, in the heart of East Africa, she discovered her love for storytelling at a very young age. What began as a hobby quickly evolved into a passion for her. During her high school years, she realized it was a gift and began writing seriously, a journey that continues to this day.

Publishing a book has always been her dream, and she is overjoyed to share it with others. She hopes that readers enjoy exploring the words created by her imagination as much as she enjoyed bringing them to life.

Contents

Chapter I:
Is it Love?

I take a sip of my wine then I put it on my nightstand. I just finished watching a very tense romance movie; it just turned me on, making me horny. I always do this to myself when I don't have anyone to calm me down. I reach down and open the drawer, get my vibrator that I bought three months ago, and start massaging my private parts. It's not the same with fucking a man, but it works for me now. After a few minutes, I get the release I was looking for, then I walk to the restroom, clean up, and go back to bed, trying to sleep.

My name is Leoncia Gregory; I am a single mother of two beautiful kids. I live alone with my kids, and I have support from my loving mother, who loves me and my kids unconditionally. My Auntie, my mother's only sister, shipped me a dildo for my twenty-fifth birthday, and it was so big that I decided to buy myself a vibrator, which works for me perfectly.

I try to sleep unsuccessfully; tomorrow is Saturday I have nothing to do. I know my mother will take the kids in the morning, and I will be alone as usual. I take my phone and open Facebook. So, I made my Facebook account when I turned eighteen; it was my first social media account. I never use it; I don't post any pictures or do any activities. One of my colleagues mentioned that it has a dating app option on it. Two months ago, I created an account with the name Leo; everybody I know calls me by the name Cia and not Leo. I put some of my best pictures, my profile looks really good. I have a chart with a couple of people, but as usual, nothing comes out of it.

I go to likes, browse a couple of names, and then I come across this profile. Wow! The guy is handsome; he has only three pictures. In the first picture, which made me check him twice, he is standing wearing a white shirt and blue jeans. He is bold; his eyes, I couldn't tell you their colors, but they look dark, maybe they are brown. His lips look so good perfect size to kiss. He is masculine; I can tell he exercises. He looks so good. In another picture, he is sitting on top of the street benches. He has brown pants and a black sweater with sunglasses. The third picture shows him sitting on a motorcycle, holding a phone. The pictures are amazing; he looks so good.

The profile says he is 6.1 feet tall and is thirty-four years old, older than the guys I have dated before, but that's not a problem for me. It says no kids; he wants a long-term relationship, smoking never, that's good. He is catholic. Well, since my ex, Pablo, I haven't been looking or considering a catholic man being a base, but it's a plus that he is.

After I check him up for a few minutes, I click the heart sign, and it shows that we matched, and I can send him a text. 'Hi! How are you?' I browsed more profiles then I fell asleep.

I wake up in the morning so tired, but my daughter is crying so much, and I know she is hungry. I pick her first from her room, and then I get her brother. Antonio is a very calm baby; he doesn't cry, he is patient, and he always does what he is told. Liliana is the opposite of him; she doesn't listen, and she always does something if she is out of sight. I swear, if I had her before Antonio, I would probably have only her. Liliana is a birth control herself.

My mother came around ten and took them; I did some cleaning and laundry for the rest of the day. My mother texted me that she would bring the kids tomorrow. I know she would stay with them, but I can't complain; I need the help and a break from them anyway.

I order some food (not in the mood to cook), and I open a new wine. I try to drink only on weekends because I have to drive my kids to school every morning. I am not an alcoholic, though I can drink a lot, especially if I am watching a movie in silence. I grabbed my food and wine and took them to the bedroom, and I ate while watching my movie.

I remember the guy I saw on Facebook yesterday. His name is Scott. I pulled my phone from my nightstand. I open Facebook and I have a text from him.

'Hey! Gorgeous.'

'How is your day going?'

I find two texts from Scott, 'Hi! My day is great.' I answer him.

'Just curious, are these pictures of you real?' He asked.

I smile and go back to my profile; I have five beautiful pictures of myself. I look so beautiful; in one of the pictures, I am wearing a red skintight trouser with a black bodysuit and a white blazer; I am standing in front of waterfalls. The second one, I was in a wedding ceremony; I was wearing a short, tight red dress. The dress hugs my body perfectly; it has a very deep neckline that covers only half of the breast while the top side of the boobs is on full display. In the third picture, I was at a football game; I was wearing jeans and a jersey, standing outside the stadium. In the other two pictures, I was wearing a cream jumpsuit, and the other is a green dress.

'They are real one hundred percent, dear.' I text back, smiling; I get that sometimes people wonder if my ass and boobs are real because they are big, not the regular size you think of.

'You are so beautiful,' He texts back.

'And you are so handsome; that's why I had to say hi when I saw you the first time.' I texted the guy is fine. I smile as a text comes in from him.

'It's a bummer we are so far from each other.' He texted back; my smile died, thinking I didn't remember where he was from. I open his profile and check again. Sure enough, there it is, Lancaster, New Hampshire.

I open Google Search and enter the USA map, and my eyes widen. He is so far from Houston; I thought I filtered my search for only a few miles. What am I going to do? The guys that seem interesting are miles away; I know I can't have a long-distance relationship.

'Yeah! It's bad, I like you,' I texted back with a cry emoji.

'We can keep talking, I don't mind. We can be friends or something.' He texted.

I send some smiley emojis.

From that day, we keep texting in the morning, sometimes in the middle of the day. A few days later, we were texting almost all the time. Then he asked me for my number; I gave it to him without thinking twice. I really hope he doesn't turn out to be like the other men on online dating who send their body parts pictures immediately after you give them your number. It will be so disappointing if he turns out to be one of those kinds of people who feel like their private parts are the only thing they can offer.

He surprised me as we started chatting; our conversation was mostly about how our day went and what we were doing. I learned he is in the real estate business, doing well in New Hampshire; he has no kids, never married. He is so perfect, but still, he lives far, so far that I know I can't start anything with him. A long-distance relationship is unrealistic for me now with two kids. It's crazy to date, even within the same city now. This is impossible. But we can keep on being friends; I need a friend, after all.

A month has passed since I started chatting with Scott; he texted me today in the morning asking if he could call me later. We hadn't talked before, even after I gave him my number; he just texted me. I am so anxious; I am not sure why he wants to talk to me. I go through the day doing my routine of the day and try not to think about the call.

The thing is, somehow, Scott has already managed to cloud my mind with thoughts about him. He is so thoughtful, attentive, and funny, plus so respectful, and I can feel that he adores me through his text. The fact that he is all that and we are just friends makes me curious how nice it will be if we are dating, but I know better not to entertain that thought.

After I put the babies to sleep, I got in my room. I sit on the bed and grab my phone. I call Scott. He picks up two rings. "Hallo! Beautiful."

I freeze as I feel something familiar but electrified through my whole body. His voice is deep and sexy; I never expected him to sound like this. He has the most amazing voice I have ever heard before.

"Leo, are you still there?" He asks when I get completely speechless.

"Hi! I am here," I say, coming out of my zoning out.

"How are you, baby girl?"

"Your voice is so fucking amazing. Jesus! It's so sexy," I say, stunned at how beautiful his voice is.

"I am pretty sure Jesus' name was not supposed to be in that sentence." We both laughed; even the way he laughed vibrated my inside. My God, he is perfect; he just turns me on with his voice. Crazy, I know. Maybe I am as horny as fuck, or my body is just responding crazily for the first time in my life.

"Can I tell you a secret?" I ask him.

"Tell me," he answers quickly.

"Your voice is turning me on." I can't believe I said that; we are supposed to be friends, and what if he thinks I am some psycho like those guys I complain about every time? Who always thinks about talking about sex before even getting to know you? But Scott and I know each other a little bit, so it might be attractive. He stays quiet for a few seconds. "I am sorry, maybe I shouldn't say that," I say when he doesn't respond.

"Don't be sorry, darling. I don't know what's going on, but I feel like this call has united our bodies in a way I can't explain. I am also turned on; it's like my body has its own brain."

"As much as I like that, Scott, we cannot go there," I say quickly.

"I know," he says, and we stay quiet for a while, almost a minute.

"I will let you sleep. Talk to you soon."

"Okay! Goodnight." I say.

"Goodnight, darling."

After that night, Scott kept calling me, and we would talk for hours, mostly on Saturdays. We always talked throughout my morning routine. I always make sure the kids are not around when I call or pick up the phone because he doesn't know about them. I never put on my profile that I have kids, and I planned if someone decides to like me or start anything with me, having kids shouldn't be a problem for them; plus, Scott, we are friends. It shouldn't matter to him if I have kids or not.

It has been three weeks now since the night we talked for the first time, and it just gets better. His voice keeps sounding sexier and hotter. I had to masturbate with my little vibrator a couple of times after he ended the call. I know it's crazy, and it doesn't help that he is super sexy.

It is Saturday, and I don't have the kids, so I pick up his calls as usual.

"Hallo! Darling," he calls me darling nowadays.

"Hi! How is your day going? "

"Perfect," I say, massaging my left breast; I always touch myself during the call.

"Can I video call you? I need to see you." His voice was deeper, and he said it slowly.

"Scott."

"I promise no funny business, it's just I need to see the woman who is stealing my heart." I freeze for a second with those words.

"That's not true." I protest, not believing what he says because I know he is stealing mine with each call.

"I am not sure exactly with the truth. But you are all I think about; I never expected to connect with you this much. Please let me see you," he is begging me, and I know I can't say no, not when I feel the same.

"Okay, call me in fifteen minutes." I did not let him answer, and I hung up. I run to the bathroom and freshen up a little. I take off my bonnet, comb my hair, and tie it in a high ponytail. I wash my face and check my teeth, making sure I don't have any food on them, even if I ate a few hours ago. I change to black shorts and a T-shirt, not forgetting to put on my bra. I do not always wear a bra inside the house. I go to my living room and wait impatiently on my couch.

I jumped when my phone rang; I touched my face faster, making sure it was clean before I picked it up. His face appeared first, then he pulled it back, and I could see him up to his chest. I can see his eyes looking at me; they are so beautiful. He has gray eyes and a long, straight nose; his lips are the perfect size for me. I can see myself kissing them. His skin looks healthy and perfect. He is so handsome; He is wearing a shirt with his buttons open with a t-shirt inside. My God, he is bold, no hair on his head; I have never dated a bald man before. He has a little mustache and a few hairs around his mouth and under his chin that are shaved lower, making him look more perfect. We stay silent for a few minutes, just looking at each other.

"You are so beautiful; my God, you are perfect." He said, looking at me as if I were the most beautiful thing he had ever seen.

"You are the perfect one; your pictures didn't even do you justice," I said, and he smiled.

"Can I see your full body, with your clothes on, of course?" We both laughed, and then I stood and put my phone on the dining table in front of the flower vase I had on top. I stand a little bit far enough for him to see me up to my thighs. He put one of his hands under his chin, massaging it slowly while checking me out. I smiled and then laughed because of the serious face he was making, like I had just dropped in front of him from an imaginary world.

"I am sorry to ask you this, is that ass and those breasts real?" I smile. That's not news to me; I have been asked the same question so many times.

Growing up, I used to hate my breast and ass because they were getting bigger compared to other parts of my body, while all my friends were flat or medium. It made me feel different and ugly for a while. Then, when men started to be attracted to them, I started liking them, but still, I can't say they are the best part of my body. I love my face more, and I believe it's beautiful; with the dimples on my cheeks, it's a plus.

"I told you they are real," I answer, smiling,

"Well, now I think we need to meet at least once." He said, surprising me.

"Scott," I call his name, sitting down.

"Only once, no strings attached. Please, Leo, you are a once-in-a-lifetime kind of human being. Let me meet you." I looked at him, begging with his beautiful eyes. "I know you don't see a future between us, and it's okay, but there is a reason we are here today. Let's meet, then leave everything to fate."

"Scott, there is a reason that you don't know; that's why this will never work as well as it is," I say, a tear rolling down my cheeks.

"Please don't cry, darling." I wipe my tears as he says that. "Let me promise you one thing: I will never force you to do anything never. Just let me meet you, and we can spend one day or two together. You can come here, or I will come to you." I look at him, tempted. Who wouldn't? I have in front of me in a video call an amazing man asking for 24 to 48 hours of my life with no strings and no promises.

Years ago, I would jump and go, but not after what I had experienced before. There is still a broken part inside me that is clouded with the doubt that breaks my heart. The doubt that I am not good enough, that it is not possible to love and be loved again, with two kids tagging along for the rest of my life. It broke me once when I had to choose them before my happiness, and I know I will do the same if I have to, but what I don't know is if I can still choose to be happy and be there for my kids at the same time. I was told before that when you are a mother, the happiness of your children comes first.

I like this man so much; I can say it's love, but what if I am not enough for him? What if I can't be who he expects me to be? What if I can't be the woman he needs? What if I am not worth it? This will be a long-distance relationship, and I have tried that before. It's not easy, especially when there are kids involved.

"Listen, my friend has a destination wedding coming up in two weeks in Miami. Come, let's have fun and leave everything to fate. What do you think?" I look at him, not knowing what to say.

"I never thought this video call would end up with a wedding invitation," I say, smiling, and he laughs. Even his laugh is sexy. Scott thinks I am a once in a lifetime, but he is the one who is once in a lifetime. I really don't want to test my fate and hurt my heart once more, but this is different. There are no expectations, no commitment, no obligation, much more, nothing to break if it doesn't work out, and the possibility of that is higher. I look at him and smile, "Okay! I will come. Send me the date information so I can book a flight."

"No, baby girl, you are my guest. I will pay for everything. Just send me your information, and I will get back to you when I get the tickets." Okay, he wants to pay for my flight, that's a free vacation.

"Okay! I will send it to you."

"Wow! I am so excited."

"Your friend will be okay with you bringing someone he doesn't know?" I ask, concerned. I don't want to be the party crusher.

"I have a plus one, and as far as I know, my friends won't mind seeing me with the most beautiful woman in this world," he says, smiling.

"I am flattered, thanks," I say, and we talk a little more for a few minutes, then end the call.

I sent him my Driving license, and then I started to panic. I just shared with a stranger one of my important documents of myself. What if he uses it to scam me or hurt me, shit this is bad. I decide to call him.

"Hallo! I received it; I will process the booking in a few hours," he says calmly.

"I don't mean to offend you, but I am going crazy that you have access to my Driving license. I hope you don't scam me." I said, going straight to the point. He laughed for a few seconds, then said.

"It's fair to worry, I am not offended," he said, and then I received a text from him with his Driving license. "There you have mine, so if I scam, you know how to find me." We laughed, then said goodbye and hung up.

The next day, he sent me the tickets to go and return. I will be arriving around 8 am on a Saturday two weeks from now, and I will leave the next afternoon around 4 pm. This means I will leave here early and come back late, but it is okay. I know my mother won't have a problem staying with the kids.

Today is the day; two weeks passed really quick. I am not complaining; finally, I will get to meet Scott in person. I am going through a lot of feelings, and I am not sure what will happen, but I am concentrating on having fun and escaping reality for thirty-plus hours of my life.

I did not tell anyone I was meeting Scot for the first time. My family knows I am going to the destination wedding in Miami of one of my friends from high school. My mother was willing to stay with the kids; the way my mother loved my kids, it was like they were hers. I swear, sometimes I feel she loves them more than me; maybe it's because she didn't have an option but to love me as her only kid, and I enjoy and love that she gets to bond with my kids the way she did with me. My mother is the best. I pray to be more like her every day with my kids.

I landed a little earlier than planned, and when I texted him, he was not at the airport yet. I take my suitcase, which is only a small carry-on, and a big purse. I didn't bring a lot of clothes. I know I will be here for a short period of time. I stand at the gates where the pickup point is waiting; I have no idea what car he is driving. I just texted him what I am wearing, which is a brown sweater jumpsuit that hugs my body really well. I know I look good, but I am still nervous; it's December and a little chilly in Houston when I left, but it's warmer here, which I should have known.

A car parked right in front of me as I was still thinking about my choice of outfit, and here he was. He parked the car, which is a white Mercedes-Benz. I smiled when he got out and walked towards me, smiling, too. He is wearing black pants and a light blue t-shirt with a collar. The three buttons are loose, showing a little of his upper chest and a full display of his long neck. He looks more handsome and sexy than his pictures; he is so yummy. He hugs me, putting one of his hands around my shoulder to my upper back and the other around my waist. I just put one of mine around his waist; the other one is holding my purse.

"My God, you are so beautiful," he says, letting go as he looks at my face, still holding my waist, but he shifts his other hand to my head, making him hold my jaw while his two fingers are massaging my cheeks. We looked at each other for like few seconds, and he closed the gap and kissed me on the mouth. I open my lips, giving his tongue access to my mouth. The kiss is slow and sweet. I have been kissed before in so many amazing ways, but when our lips met, it was like a force of magnet going through my body, and I could feel the eruption of the butterfly in my stomach going through all my veins. It's an amazing feeling that can be addictive, the one that makes you forget your own name.

The car behind him honked and brought us back to reality; he let go of my neck, placed his hands on my waist, and buried his head on my neck, smelling me with his nose. "Can you move your car?" Someone says behind us, while the other driver starts honking aggressively.

Scott holds my hand to the other side, opening the door for me. Then he goes around and puts my bag in the trunk, then he gets in and starts driving. I don't recognize the smell of the fragrance he has on, but it smells so good.

"I apologize; some people are so impatient," he said, driving us out of the airport.

"I know, so do you." We both smile.

"Yeah! I try not to, but you make it harder," he said, smiling.

He drove us to the hotel where we would stay. So his friends have rented a mansion on Airbnb, but Scott took a hotel for us; he said he did not want me to feel uncomfortable. But I think it's mostly because he wanted to be only us tonight after the wedding, which I can't complain about after the kiss we shared; I am counting down the minutes till I kiss his soft lips again. This weekend, I decided before I left home that I was going to enjoy myself and forget about everything and anything holding me back. It's going to be the weekend to remember.

Scott already checked in yesterday, even if he didn't sleep in, so I will be able to get in today and get ready. He is one of the groomsmen, so he has to go and get ready with the rest of the groomsmen where the wedding is happening. So, I had to get ready right away after we got to the hotel because the ceremony was starting in three hours.

"I will send someone to pick you up when you're ready," he said, moving my carry-on inside.

"Okay!" I say, smiling as he comes close to me. I close my eyes as he holds my face with his two hands, then he kisses me again. The kiss is slow and passionate; I have been longing to be kissed this way for years. Scott is so perfect and an amazing kisser that it makes me think how he is in bed; he is driving me insane already.

"I have to go," he said in my mouth when he let go of the kiss. He says it more to him rather than me.

"Okay! I will see you later." I say, looking at his beautiful face.

"Yes, see you," he opened the door and left.

I started getting ready immediately after he left; I didn't want to be late. It was already ten am, and the wedding started at 1:30 pm. I shower; straightening my hair gives it waves at the end. I have natural hair that goes down to my shoulders. After I was satisfied with my hair, I started to do my makeup.

There was a knock at the door as I started to do my eyebrows. I walk to the door and open it, "Hallow, ma'am, I have a branch here for you." The room service guy says to me, entering the room with a tray full of breakfast meals and coffee with a mimosa. I smile, thanking him as he exits the room. So, apart from being handsome, caring, and passionate now, I can add thoughtfully. He knew I didn't have breakfast, and for him to order breakfast for me is adding to how amazing he is. There are waffles, sausage, scrambled eggs, toasted bread, some salads, and extra orange juice and champagne. Then I saw a red rose with a small envelope. I open it and it's written. Enjoy your meal, beautiful. Can't wait to see you.' Scott signs his name under the message. I smile, eating a little of everything. I don't want to eat too much, I'm going to a wedding, I'm sure there is more good food there.

I finished my makeup, and I feel proud of my finished work. I put on my dress; I am wearing a long, red dress with a thin strap that runs lower down the middle of my back. The dress has a built-in bra that pushes my breasts up, leaving cleavage with half of the top of my breasts out. The dress hugs me perfectly. Also, it has a slit on my left side to the mid of my left thigh. I look at myself in the mirror, proud of how I look. I started to work out two years ago, and I have lost the baby fat from my babies, and I know I look pretty good.

I texted Scott that I was ready, and he ordered Uber to pick me up and take me to the venue. I get there, and the wedding is taking place at the beach; the stage where the bride, groom, bridesmaids, and groomsmen will stand is made on top of the water, and all the guests are sitting on the shore where there are chairs lined up in two parts. A man stops me at the staged entrance, "Excuse me, what's your name?" I forgot Scott told me they would ask for my name.

"I am Leoncia Gregory, plus one of Scott Anderson's," I answered as he told me to say.

"Okay! You're welcome; please take a seat on the right side," he said, smiling.

"Thanks." I walk and sit in the middle near the Aisle where the bride will go through, wanting to see everything while I enjoy the ceremony. It's not every day I get invited to a wedding, and this one seems to be one of a kind.

"OMG! Are you Leo?" a woman older than me, maybe Scott's age, asked me, surprised, looking at me from head to toe, smiling.

"Yes?" I answer, questioning her with my eyes.

"Forgive me, I'm just stunned by your beauty. Scott said you are beautiful, but he didn't give you enough justice with his explanations," she continues, "By the way, my name is Linda. Scott is my friend, and he asks me to give you company as he gets through his groomsman's duty." I just nod and smile. It's nice of him to want me to be comfortable; Linda seems nice and mesmerized by my beauty. I hope we will have fun.

"Okay!" I manage to say.

"You look so beautiful; I swear you put all the girls here except the bride to shame. I am straight, but girl, I would date you if I weren't. I hope Scott realizes how lucky he is," she said, smiling at me.

"Trust me, I'm the lucky one," I said as they started walking in front of the ceremony as it started. I see Scott getting in with a lady; everyone here looks beautiful and rich. I am glad I wear this dress, it's beautiful and classic.

The ceremony was beautiful; Scott was looking at me all the time he was standing in front. Linda and I moved to the other venue where the reception will be held. "This is so beautiful," I say, looking at the place; everything is beautiful.

Linda smiled at me excitedly when I felt two strong hands wrapped around my waist from behind me; I knew it was Scott before he placed his lips on my ear and said, "You look absolutely stunning." I smiled.

I turn around and hug him, "You look amazing too."

"Are you enjoying, or is she boring you?" He asks, smiling,

"She is perfect," I say, turning around to face Linda.

"Do you guys still need an introduction?" He asks.

"No, we are fine," Linda answers.

"Okay! I still have some groomsman duties to finish. I will come to you as soon as I can," he said.

"Take your time; she is perfectly fine here," Linda says, and we both smile before Scott walks back outside.

The reception was amazing, as expected. Scott came and sat with us when it was time to eat. He introduced me to some of his friends, too. He came and picked me up when it was time to dance, and the MC announced everyone could come and dance with the bride and groom.

We slowly dance, holding each other. He kisses me several times, a closed-mouth kiss. I am really enjoying myself in his arms, feeling as safe as I ever felt before. I know at this point, there is something more, something I may never be able to control. He makes me feel things I never felt before; he is so perfectly imperfect for me. And I have no idea how this night will end.

We left as soon as the reception ended and the bride and groom left. Scott drives us straight to the hotel. We didn't say anything on the way here; he was just kissing my hand, which he held all the way, making me feel comfort I had never experienced before.

We go straight to the room when we get to the hotel. Scott spun me around and pinned me to the wall as soon as he closed the door. He took off his jacket and started unbuttoning his shirt, and I helped him in the process. He let it fall down, leaving his hard, beautiful chest bare; I traced my hand through it to his stomach before he closed the gap between us and started kissing me mercilessly. My legs are between his long ones; I put my hands on his bald head. It's so soft. Then I heard the sound of a fabric being torn apart; I opened my eyes and was surprised to see that Scot had ripped my dress apart in the middle of my stomach. My breasts come flying out, my nipples so hard they hurt.

"Ooh! My God, you ruined my dress." I said breathlessly, turned on as I had never been before.

"Don't worry, I will buy you another one." He said to my ears, cupping his hand on my breast and pinching my hard nipples, driving me crazy; I moaned so loud, releasing the pressure I felt with his hand's magic.

He released my breasts as he kept kissing me; his hand traveled lower down my back to my ass, squeezing it while pushing me towards him, making me feel his hard penis inside his pants. He rubbed it against the front part of my pussy. I close my eyes as he travels his lips down my neck, kissing it so hard I know it will leave a mark.

He cups one of my breasts again before he sucks almost half of it with his mouth, "Scott, oh! My God, Yeeeeees!" I scream so loud, pressing my head back towards the wall with my hands holding his head. He keeps doing what he is doing unbothered, moving from one breast to another until I start shaking, experiencing my first orgasm with Scott just by him sucking my breast.

He released my breasts and kneeled down between my legs; he pulled down my dress with the thong I was wearing underneath. He looks at me naked in front of him as we lock eyes while mine are half closed because I am still on the high from the orgasm he gave me a few moments ago. He pulls one of my legs and puts my feet on his shoulder, making my pussy exposed in front of him. I lose my balance a little, so I hold the couch nearby while putting my other hand on his shoulder, making me bend a little and exposing myself to him even more. In a split second, he buried his mouth in my clit, holding both my ass cheeks under to give me balance. He eats me up like candy or corn. He eats as if his life depended on it. I moaned so loud that I called his name, begging him not to stop, and he didn't until he felt me so close to exploding. He stands up, kissing me on the mouth. He unbuckles his belt pushing his pants down, and within a few seconds, he pulls one of my legs to his waist, sliding his penis inside me like a hungry snake. He felt so good, and my body started shaking with pressure. Then I exploded in a few minutes, but it didn't stop him. He kept thrusting in and out through my orgasm while building my desires up, and we kept going until we both reached climax together, and he exploded inside of me. Scott and I never talked about this before this trip. I knew I would have sex with him, and I was ready for it, but this is out of this world. He is giving me what I have been looking for to be loved, cherished, and fucked right. I know by now that I am in deep shit.

He holds my hand and leads me to the bathroom; I sit down on the edge of the bathtub as he removes all the makeup on my face, which is ruined in so many ways. I removed some makeup on his face, too, that was transferred to him from my face. We get under the shower and start showering each other. Scott turned me around after we rinse the soap off our bodies, then he bends me a little as I hold the shower handle, and he slide inside me again fucking me under the shower hard and passionately. He feels as good as he holds and squeezes my breast from behind. I swear, the way my body responds to him, it's like I have known him all along. "You feel so good, baby girl. I can't stop myself; you're so fucking hot," he said into my ears breathlessly.

"Then don't stop." I hear myself say breathlessly, too.

We move to the bed and fuck so many times in different styles, missionary, doggie style, we stand, I sit on his lap, cowgirl, and so many I don't remember all. We change and repeat them in between orgasms. We had so much fun, and we finally fell asleep in the morning as the sun started rising. As I lay there under the sheets with my head on Scott's chest, with him wrapping his arm around me to the side of my breast. I can't help but remember one man I truly loved in the past. The only difference, the biggest one, is that Scott is way better than him on so many levels. He is fucking amazing, and if it was not clear before, it's clear that I am falling harder, and I have no idea what to do. He wasn't supposed to be like this; for the first time, I hoped the sex would turn out bad, but now I am not even sure if we were only fucking; it felt more like we were making love passionately at the highest level that I have ever experienced before. I fall asleep shortly because I am so exhausted.

I wake up first before Scott. He is sleeping peacefully; the sheets cover only half of his body. He looks so cute sleeping; I trace his chest with my fingers. He shifts a little but does not wake up. I need him to wake up; it's almost time for me to leave, and I need to feel him inside me one more time. I take the sheet off him and place myself in between his legs, then I hold his penis and put it inside my mouth, giving him the best blow job I could master. He wakes up in seconds; I can feel him become hard in a few minutes. He holds my hair, pushing my head more as I take his length in all the way to my throat. I know that felt better as he groans, turning me more on beyond my wildest imagination.

He moves up, pulling my body up then he comes on top of me, spreading my legs open before he pushes his penis inside my wet pussy. He thrusted inside and out of me while kissing me everywhere, from my lips, neck, cheeks, and breasts, driving me even crazier. I moan so loud, releasing the pressure in the process as we reach climax together. He pulls me to his lap, still inside me, and he looks me in the eyes and says. "Leo, can you please be my girlfriend?"

"What?" I ask, surprised.

"Look, I know you have your reasons why this may not work, but I promise you, I will do whatever I can to make this work." I get off him and move to the other side. "Tell me…

yesterday, this morning, what happened now doesn't mean anything. Because for me, it's everything I have been looking for, and you should know I am in love with you, Leo," he said, holding my hands. We are both naked, and his body is so distracting to me right now.

"Scott, I have a lot going on; all this is so tempting. I know I am falling too, but I don't know…. I am scared." I said, tears coming down my cheeks.

"Why are you scared?" He asks, holding my cheeks with his hands.

"Would you want to date a single mother with two kids already?"

He looks at me, confused. "What do you mean?" He asks, not understanding me.

"Scott, I have two kids, my kids. They stay with me twenty-four-seven. Do you still want me to be your girlfriend?" I stood up and put a towel around me.

"Why didn't you tell me you have kids?" He asks angrily; I have never seen him angry before.

"Because I did want you to love me beyond any reasonable doubt, "I say, not even believing it myself. I still don't know exactly why I never shared my kids with him before today.

"That's bullshit, and you know it. You and I have been talking for some time, and you didn't think I should know something like that?" He asks again.

"I am sorry; this was not supposed to end with you asking me to be your girlfriend," I said, the obvious.

"So you decided to lie to me because we had no future. Leo, you have kids, that's not something you lie about."

"I didn't lie. I just did not say it, but it doesn't mean I am a liar," I said, raising my voice.

He looks at me and then says, "How do you expect me to trust you after this?"

"So now you think you can't trust me. Is that it, or is it because you found out I have kids already?"

"Leo, you are so amazing and adorable. Falling for you is so easy, but now I don't think I want to be in a relationship with someone I don't trust," he said, then added, "This is not a small thing to lie about."

"That's where you are wrong, Scott; I never told you I don't have kids. You assumed I didn't. And I don't share with everyone I meet about my children. Plus, you and I were not supposed to be talking about this or about them." I said I hoped he would rethink and understand my point; I hoped this didn't end before it even started.

"Yeah! I forgot that I am just someone insignificant; isn't that why you insisted we were not meant to be? Well, your wishes are granted, Leo. Whatever this was, it is over." The tears escape my eyes. I walk to the bathroom and lock it. I cry silently as I shower, knowing the small hope that was building up is over.

Scott is sitting on the couch wearing his boxers only when I get out. I went straight to my suitcase; I did not unpack anything, so I just looked for the outfit I planned to wear and started getting ready. Scott goes to the bathroom. By the time he gets out, I am ready to go. I pick up my phone and open the Uber app, ready to call for one, when he says. "I will take you to the airport."

"You don't have. I can manage." I say while I enter the address. He grabs my phone and exits the app.

"I was the one who invited you here; I will make sure you get to the airport safely." I took my phone back, then I sat on the couch, waiting for him to get ready.

He drives me to the airport, I look outside the whole time, and he concentrates on the road. None of us says anything. He helps to take my bag out and opens the door. I take my things and start leaving.

"Leo, it was nice to see you," he said before I turned around, and I didn't say anything. I just pulled my bag inside, leaving him standing out there.

I am one hour early; I just checked in, then I sit on the benches waiting for the time to board. This trip took a lot of turns, making me remember what my life has made me go through; my life has been a big disappointment for years. I don't seem to find the right partner for my life. It's always something; I don't know what to do. Yes, I have kids, but does that make me less attractive? I have men and women praise my beauty when they see me, but how come this beauty can't get a man who will stay and be with me beyond anything? The only man who loved me like that couldn't make me feel worthy, and when I thought I had found someone who made me feel more like a woman and not a mother of two kids, I messed up. I try to think about how far my life has come to this point.

Chapter II:
Young and in Love

A few years ago

As you already know, my name is Leoncia Gregory, my friends and family call me Cia. I am a black American born to an African woman from East Africa, Tanzania, and an American man from Detroit, Michigan. They met in Houston, Texas, got married, and then moved to Dallas. I was raised in a loving and peaceful household, having a normal childhood that all kids deserve. I lost my dad to a car accident when I was sixteen, and my life changed. It was never the same again.

For a year, we moved in with my grandparents in Detroit until my mother got a new job back in Houston, Texas, and we moved back to the city where I was born. As a seventeen-year-old, shy, nerdy girl, it was hard to make new friends. Other than my neighbor Teresa, aka Tessa, I had no friends. Thank God Tessa had a couple of friends from the school we both went to, and she introduced me to some of them. I joined some of the clubs in school, and I joined the art club, that's where I met Pablo, my first boyfriend.

Pablo and I started as friends, we spent most of our time at school together… with Tessa, of course. Until he told me on our homecoming celebration that he was in love with me. I was so happy because I loved him back. We had our first kiss that night, and agreed to be a couple.

Two weeks later, we had sex for the first time. It was his birthday; he was turning 18 years old. His parent had a little celebration at their home for him, and all his friends showed up. Pablo was Hispanic from Colombia but, like me, was born and raised in the United States. His mom loved me so much and was excited to have her first daughter-in-law. Pablo had two more brothers: Daniel, who was 12 years old, and the youngest, Carlos, who was 7 years old.

Pablo was so cute, and as he transitioned to a real man, he looked hotter every day. I was so proud to be his girlfriend, and I didn't think twice about being with him that night when we snuck into his bedroom. Our first was not that great because it was trial and error. I remember him pushing like three times unsuccessfully to try entering through my pussy. When he finally did, I cried in pain, and he got scared and stopped. I seriously thought I only lost half of my virginity that day, and we decided to learn more about it before we tried again.

I went and asked Aunt Juliet, my mother's only sister, about virginity, and she explained a little. Pablo also asked his Aunt Valeria, who was his mother's friend's little sister, but for some reason, she was close to Pablo. He sometimes went out with her to parties. I knew Pablo and his brothers sometimes used to stay with her when their parents were on vacation or out having some time alone.

Two weeks later, I went to Pablo's house and we got to his room. His parents went out for his brother's football practice, and it was just us alone. We try to have sex again. We both took our clothes off and I lied down on the bed. Pablo moved on top of me and spread my legs, then he pushed his dick inside my pussy in one thrust and I moaned with pleasure. It was painful, and how my body felt was like nothing I had felt before. He started moving his hips in and out for some time, then we both moaned hard as he exploded inside me, and it felt amazing. It was our first orgasm and the best one.

From that day, Pablo and I kept fooling around, and we sometimes had sex while his mother was downstairs staring at the cooking.

One day, she came inside Pablo's room and found us naked under the covers. We were not fucking but Pablo was kissing my boobs in the process of turning me on. "What are you guys doing?" She was terrified, and we were more embarrassed for being caught. She drove me back home and told my mother about us. I remember that night my mother had a talk with me, telling me all the negative things that can happen from having sex at my age; pregnancy, and HIV were the main topics.

From that day, Pablo and I were not allowed to close our room if we were in it together. All we could do was kiss only on the lips, but it was okay for us; we loved each other either way.

Days, then months passed, and it was almost time for prom. Pablo surprised me at the cafeteria with his fellow music club members. It was the only club that we didn't share because I can't sing. He came seconds after I sat and started eating, and they started to sing and dance a serenade to me in front of the entire school, with a sign that said '*CAN YOU BE MY PROM DATE?*' I said yes, and everybody cheered for us.

My mother cried so much that day when I showed her the video. She couldn't believe I had grown up to be a young lady who was asked on dates, which was hard for her to do. I am her only baby, and she was a single mother and a widow trying to survive with a teenager.

I remember my prom day like it happened yesterday; I felt like one of the most beautiful girls in the world. I am very curvy, my hips are wide and I have a big ass. Plus, my breasts are full, round, and cannot fit in a hand (one of the things I knew Pablo loved about my body). I have chocolate black skin that's so soft. I know my face is beautiful, but my secret weapon is my brown eyes, dimples on both cheeks, and my full lips. I got a lot of compliments when I was young, but on my prom day, it was over the top. I wore a long red dress with a slit on my left side that came to my thigh. The armless dress hugged me so well; my hair was tied down in a ponytail. My mom took me to the salon, and they did my hair and makeup. I also put on black heels. For sure, I looked beautiful like a snack. My mother gave me her gold jewelry set that my dad bought for her a few days before his death, including two beautiful butterfly earrings, a chain with a little butterfly pendant in the middle, and a beautiful bracelet. I looked stunning, older. I sure felt amazing and confident.

Pablo picked me up in a Mercedes-Benz, which is his dad's, and I felt like a princess being picked up by the prince charming himself. Pablo was my prince charming; he was wearing a tuxedo, and his hair was shaved perfectly. He looked amazing. The prom was a blast; we ended up having a lot of fun.

The prom celebration was amazing; the fact that this was our last high school celebration before graduation made it so memorable.

We left early because Pablo's cousin had a house party. Pablo and I crashed the party after prom. When we got inside, there were a lot of grown-ups in their mid-twenties and older. There was alcohol. Pablo gave me a glass of alcohol. I don't even know what's in it; it tasted good, and I liked it. After a few minutes, he pulled me upstairs to an unoccupied room because there were people everywhere. I knew exactly what he wanted, and I wanted it too, so after he locked the door, we did not waste any time. In few minutes we were on the bed having amazing sex, and as any horny teenagers would, we completely forgot about the condoms which my mother always put in my school bag. She made sure to put a packet in my purse; I know Pablo got some of them from his mom too.

He took me home after that. I went straight to my room after I greeted my mother and told her how beautiful and amazing the prom was. I also showed her the pictures I took on my phone, making sure I never mentioned the house party. She was already not happy with the fact that I was late when I got home, but because it was prom night, she let it slide.

My mother and I are somehow close; I tell her a lot of things. I remember I told her when Pablo and I met, and how I thought he was the most handsome man on the planet. Still, it was so hard for me to open up to her about my sex life because no matter how close we were, she was still my mother, and no one tells their mother how good sex is; they aren't even supposed to know we are having sex.

Three weeks later, we graduated. Our graduation was on Thursday; my family took me to dinner. My grandparents from my father's side came, my mother's mother also came, my auntie Juliet, my mother's little sister, and some of my mother's friends were guests too. The place was filled with neighbors and friends, including Pablo and his mother. It is a celebration of around thirty people. I had so much fun. My aunt let me taste her wine, but we kept this a secret from my mother. My Auntie is ten years younger than my mother; she was fifteen when I was born, so sometimes she feels like the sister I never had.

Pablo's parent were throwing a party for him on Saturday, and I was invited. We were both so happy to be done with high school. We were both accepted at (UHD) University of Houston Downtown. I couldn't wait to spend my college years with the love of my life.

I woke up the next day sick, I was throwing up and having diarrhea, also I had a hut ban a really bad one. I couldn't eat anything, so my mother bought Pedialyte solution and some over-the-counter medication to help me get better. The diarrhea stopped, and I felt a bit better. I was able to eat soup successfully.

On Saturday, I woke up more sick and weak. At around 10 am, my mother decided to take me to the emergency room. We all thought it was food poisoning because I had eaten a lot of food the day before I got sick. At that time, everything was so tasty, but when I got sick, nothing tasted good.

When we got to the hospital, they put an IV drip for me to get rehydrated while they ran some tests. After some time, I don't know how long, the doctor came and took my mother out of the room. When they came back, my mother had tears in her eyes, and my heart started to beat fast. I hoped I didn't have some critical condition or something. "Leoncia! When was the last time you got your period?" The doctors asked me.

"Last month." The truth is, I was not sure, but I was not about to tell them.

"Well, the test shows that you are pregnant."

I looked at the doctor like he had grown an extra head. 'No. No. No. No.' I freaked out on the inside; when I turned to look at my mother, I saw a single tear rolling down her cheek. I knew very well it was not a happy tear, at least not for now. She had so many talks with me about this; my mother had me when she was 25, so to make her a grandma at 43 was not flattering at all.

"I recommend you find a pediatrician as soon as possible; I can refer you to one." The doctor said, looking at me, then he turned and looked at my mother. "After that IV is out, you should be okay to leave. The nurse will be here with you shortly." Then he left.

My mother looked at me, and I couldn't raise my head to look at her. I felt scared, well, terrified, and I knew I had disappointed my mother so much. "What, it's one thing not to listen to what I have said to you a number of times, but this is reckless. You know, it may not be only the pregnancy that you have? Did you even use those condoms I gave you?" I just shook my head. I was so embarrassed.

Two hours later, I was discharged, and we got home at around 9 pm. At this point, Pablo was at his graduation party with his family and some of our friends, celebrating. I already texted him that I was sick and was unable to make it. He called me worried, but I assured him that I felt better.

The next day, I slept throughout the whole morning, and my mother woke me up, telling me Pablo and his parents were on their way.

We sat down in our living room, and my mother told them the news that I was expecting. Pablo didn't seem bothered that much, and his dad was not angry but sad. His mother's reaction was the same as my mother's. They both remind us that they had tried so hard to avoid this situation.

"Now that you two have decided to become parents, I propose you should get married." Mr. Martin Pablo's father said.

"No! I don't think that is the best idea, these two are still so young for marriage," my mother said angrily.

"Well, we are catholic, and I am not going to allow a grandchild of mine to be born in a broken family," he said, looking at my mother.

"Wait, please let us ask the children first, these things cannot be forced, Honey," Mrs. Martin said, standing in front of her husband, who was passing in front of us. He turned and looked at us, "You two love each other, right?" He asked us, and we nodded, "I need you guys to use your words." He said angrily.

"Yes." We both answered quickly.

"They have love, the baby is on the way now, we need to make a safe house for the baby. I will talk with Father Francis and set a date." Mr. Martin said, concluding.

"If we are letting them get married, it shouldn't be in church. Let them have a court marriage and then, if this goes well, they can bless their marriage in church," my mother suggested.

"I think that's a good idea for now. We both want what's best for them," Pablo's mother, Mrs. Teresa, added.

Mr. Martin looked at us one more time, then he said, "Okay! It will be a small ceremony with only family and close friends."

And just like that, the date was set, Pablo's dad took us to buy the rings, and I didn't get an engagement ring. His mother and mine took me to buy a dress. We got married two months later and had a private ceremony at Pablo's parents' backyard. It was amazing and simple.

Chapter III:
Marriage

Our parents together rented us a one-bedroom apartment and paid for a first deposit while helping us to get a joint credit card that we would use and pay for going forward. Pablo started working in a construction hardware store immediately after we found out I was pregnant; I also started working at a grocery store a month after my morning sickness slowed down.

We moved into our apartment a week after the wedding. The plan was to start studying online, and we had both already enrolled for the next semester. I would be studying finance; my GPA was good, so it was not hard for me to get a nice course. I was so excited about what I was going to study. My father was an accountant, and I felt proud that I would be following in his footsteps. I had been thinking about my father lately, wondering how he would feel about me getting pregnant this young, but I guess we will never find that out.

Pablo wanted to study law, but he didn't do that well in some classes, so he decided to study an associate's degree in paralegal before he moved forward.

The marriage life for us had been challenging. I was not sure how it was supposed to be, but I was sure the pregnancy didn't make it easier anyway. Well, we managed to pick up some type of routine; Pablo had a fixed schedule, Monday to Friday, 7 am to 7 pm, twelve hours. He was going to reduce the hours when he started classes in a month; after that, he always did some Uber driving on the side. He had a car; his father gave it to him on our wedding as a gift. Mr. Martin owned a Car Shop, which sold and repaired cars. It was pretty big, and he made a really good profit. Sometimes Pablo helped his father at the shop, mostly on weekends.

I always stayed home on my free days, or I went to visit my mother. She owned a beauty supply store and did hair while renting some of the space to other hairdressers, but mostly the space was for other beauty supplies. She also did taxes during tax season, but she only had a small clientele.

Pablo sometimes picked me up and dropped me off, but most of the time I took Uber, which for me was affordable considering I lived like eight minutes from the store. When we were both off, most of the time we stayed home watching movies and making love.

When I was almost five months pregnant, for some reason, I didn't feel confident in my body. I was more tired every day and I felt bigger than usual, because aside from my belly, my boobs and ass had become bigger. I still enjoyed sex, but every time we had sex, I felt so insecure and undesirable.

I came home one day at around 8:30 pm. I had this shift the past two days. 'Thank God I'm off tomorrow so I can rest,' I thought. Pablo had been so moody those couple of days, I knew it was my fault. I had been avoiding having sex and always complaining that we would hurt the baby, knowing full well that sex wouldn't hurt the baby. But you couldn't blame me, as Pablo was never gentle with me. When he got on top of me, he would just thrust his thing in me with no care; sometimes, I felt he just had sex with me to satisfy his desires only. I don't know when our sex life changed; I used to enjoy having sex with him. What happened? I was not sure.

"Hi!" I greeted him as I went straight to the bathroom so I could take a shower, and he was sitting on the bed. I came out and he looked at me with his beautiful eyes. Those eyes, I swear, they are the ones to blame most for me getting pregnant. Pablo has the best set of eyes that can melt you down, especially when he looks at you the way he was looking at me now.

"What?" I asked, smiling because he looked so mischievous, like someone with a motive but not a good one.

"Come sit here, have you eaten?" He asked me because sometimes I ate at work, especially if I had a late shift.

"Yes," I said, wondering what's up with him.

"Okay! Come here, let me show you something."

I climbed on the bed and sat next to him; I had only a towel covering me. He took his laptop and logged in, and then he clicked on one of the files and clicked on a video. It was a video of a man and a woman having sex, and the woman was pregnant.

"What is this?" I asked in surprise.

"This is how we are going to make our life better, my love. I don't want you to think I don't care. I do… a lot. Cia, you mean everything to me now, and this baby, our baby, is the symbol of our love. We have to make each other feel better." I smiled. This meant a lot. I was ready to do anything to save our love and make our life better.

"Okay, baby, take that off." He instructed me to take off the towel, which I did. "Look at the laptop, baby, you see what he is doing, I am going to do it to you, and then you will do what she does, Okay, my love."

"Okay."

He started massaging my breasts with his hands, being extra gentle, while he kissed me on my neck, and I actually felt so good. He moved his mouth to my breast taking one after the other and sucked them using his lips more and not his teeth as he used to do before. He moved one of his hands down between my legs massaging my clit with his fingers. It made electric shocks go through my body, and I made crazy sounds involuntary. He didn't stop, though. He pushed his two fingers inside my pussy and I cried his name while my thighs closed involuntary, my breathing accelerated and I shut my eyes. I didn't know you could feel this much pressure with just fingers.

"Open your eyes for me, baby girl, look at me, Cia."

I tried to open my eyes, but they betrayed me as he thrust his finger inside and out. In a few minutes, I came hard.

"Wow!" I said, smiling.

Pablo moved up. We started kissing, and then he said. "Now it's my turn."

"Okay."

He played the video which was paused and I saw the woman putting the guy's penis in her mouth. "It's okay, try it, baby." He sat at the edge of the bed, and I knelt down between his legs. I put his penis inside my mouth, it felt weird doing it but I would do anything to make this man happy. "Use your lips and tongue baby like you're sucking a lollipop." I followed his instructions while looking at the woman in the video. After few minutes I saw Pablo enjoying what I was doing and he held my head, pushing himself deeper, fucking my mouth so hard. I smiled when he exploded all over my face and hands.

"Wow!" I said, surprised.

"You see, Cia, this is amazing."

I went to the restroom and cleaned up.

When I came back into the room, Pablo was full naked now. He had the pillows in the middle of the bed. "Come, and stay here like this." He shows me how to sit. I put my chest on the pillow and assumed a child's pose with my ass up. Then he let himself in from behind- into my pussy. I gulped with pressure; it felt so good. He positioned himself better, and he started to increase the momentum, in and out, increasing the pace with each thrust.

We both reached climax, and the orgasm was amazing. I don't know why we never tried this before. But that didn't matter anyway, now we were going to enjoy all the time.

From that day on, Pablo kept coming up with different videos. We watched and copied them, but sometimes it was too much for me. I love him, so I kept doing it for him.

Months passed by, and I gave birth to a beautiful baby boy. We call him Antonio. Pablo came up with the name, and I was okay with it. My mother stayed with us for two weeks, helping me so I could heal. Pablo was not happy about that; he had to sleep on the couch, and some days he stayed at his parents' house.

I learned a lot from her during those couple of months, and especially during the two weeks that she was there. I am so grateful to have her. I stopped working three weeks before I gave birth, and I was still going to stay for some time. I took a leave of absence.

Pablo and I hadn't been intimate for a while before I gave birth, and with my mother in the apartment, we couldn't do anything. I was breastfeeding the baby when he got back from work. He went straight to the bathroom to shower, and then he came out, looking at me.

"What?" I asked, knowing exactly what he wanted. He did not answer, and he took off the towel, leaving himself naked. Pablo was so attractive, or maybe I was biased because I loved him. He didn't exercise a lot, but his job kept him fit. He was tall for his age, not too slim, just enough for my eyes, he had just shaved his facial hair- he had a lot for his age, but the shave made him look a little bit younger, and so cute.

"Did I answer your question?" He asked, getting closer to the bed. His penis was straight, erected forward and I just gulped and put the baby in his bassinet near the bed. I had been scared to have sex for so many reasons. First, I felt so insecure with my body, and I had been a little sore down there after the baby. I still couldn't believe I had a eight-pound point something baby come out of my pussy. I am lucky he didn't tear my walls and break my pussy.

The first thing he did when he got on the bed was grab my breasts and squeeze them, which was a mistake. The milk spilled all over him.

"What the fuck?" He screamed.

"You know I am breastfeeding, my breasts are off-limits for now," I told him as he ran back to the bathroom to clean the milk. I took the paper tower and wipes from the bassinet and cleaned my breasts.

When Pablo came back, he just got into bed and spread my legs, and entered me.

"Aww!" I winced in pain as he pushed himself in, but Pablo did not care and kept going, thrusting his hips in and out. After some time, the pain eased up, and I knew better than to complain; I already knew Pablo had been patient with me, the only thing I could do was fulfill my duties as a wife.

From that day, we resumed our sex life, but it was no longer the same. Pablo did not bring the porn videos anymore but he started having sex with me aggressively. It pissed me off and turned me off all together. He, of course, did not care.

Chapter IV:
Adultery

It has been three months since the day I had my baby. I know, maybe I am biased, but Antonio is the most beautiful baby. I started working again two weeks ago. I leave my son with Pablo's mother when I go to work, and Pablo is not home. Sometimes, I will drop him off at my mother's beauty supply shop.

Pablo dropped out of college; his parent don't know yet. I told him to tell them because they have paid for this semester, which he didn't finish. He enrolled in the military, where he was accepted to join, and he will join the army soon.

Since he made that decision, he doesn't work as much, also he doesn't stay home at all. For three weeks, he has been going out every Friday night to Sunday, claiming he is going out with his friends. I know he kept some of his friends from high school, but most of them are in college, even though I know it's not impossible for him to meet them; most of them are in Houston.

Three days ago, he went to work and came back at 2 am the next morning. I called him several times he didn't pick up. Then I called his mom, and by accident, I spilled the beans, telling her that he dropped out of college. He has been so mad at me, and we are currently not on speaking terms.

He goes straight to the bathroom after he gets home. I have no idea where he is going or if he will stay in, but it's Friday and he goes out on Friday nowadays. His phone vibrated on the table. I put the baby on the bed and picked it up. The caller ID is V, just a simple V.

"P, are you already on your way?" A woman's voice says from the other side, I think I recognize it, though I have no idea who it is.

"Who is this?" I ask angrily

"Shit!" the woman says, then hangs up.

"What are you doing? Now you pick up my phone calls?" Pablo asks angrily as he catches me talking to whoever called his phone.

"Who is V?" I ask, ignoring him.

"My friend, you don't know them," he answers, taking his phone from me.

"Who is V? Are you cheating on me?" I ask him, hoping that what I feel and think is not true.

"V is my friend; I am meeting with some of my other friends. What's wrong with you? First, you snitched on me, and now you're picking up my phone calls. You need to learn boundaries."

"Boundaries! That woman should learn some first. You are my husband, and lately I wonder if you remember that." I am so mad and on the verge of crying. Pablo looks at me and comes closer to where I am standing. He puts his hands on my cheeks, holding my head.

"She is just a friend, nothing more. I am going through some self-struggles right now; I need to go out and think. I can't do it here," he says to me.

"Pablo, I am your wife, you should talk to me about your troubles, not strangers?" I say to him, holding his hands. It seems so long since the last time we touched like this, even though we sleep in the same room.

"I don't talk to them, but I need to go out. Between you and the baby's crying, I can't think straight here. Okay, see you later." He lets me go, then picks up his wallet and keys; he is already dressed.

"Please pick up my calls when I call," I say sadly.

"Stop calling, I'm okay, I will come back when I come back." He raises his voice a little, sounding annoyed. I just stood there by the door watching him leave, tears rolling down my cheeks. I can sense deep down in my gut that this V woman is more than just a friend to Pablo. If that's true, I know it will hurt me deeply.

It's three in the morning, and Pablo is not back. I called him several times he didn't pick up as usual. I decided to call his friend Jordan. They are not as close anymore as they used to but I know they hang out with common friends, and they have been in the same place before. I just want to know if he saw him.

Jordan and Pablo grew up together; they were on the football team together till Pablo stopped playing in the 10th grade. Their parents know each other; actually, their mothers are friends. I just found out like five months ago from one of our friends, Janet, that Jordan asked for my phone number. I asked why, then she told me that Jordan and Pablo both loved me and made a pact the day I started school here that if one of them got to be with me, the other person would stay away, and that's how their relationship ended. I never knew why they didn't talk anymore. Pablo told me Jordan was too busy with football and that their interests were not the same anymore.

Jordan is so good at football; he is a quarterback, and he got a full scholarship to college for that. He is so talented; I have watched his college team play several times. I know football season is over now, and he has been hanging out with his friends, including Pablo. I have called him several times in the past weeks just to know where Pablo is. I know Jordan is the only person who won't tell Pablo I called him.

The phone rings three times before he picks up. "Hallo!" His voice is so deep and sexy, I always admire it even though it doesn't do a lot to me. I am in love with Pablo. Jordan attracts attention from women who are more beautiful than I am, so I doubt he would ever be interested in me.

"I am sorry, did I wake you?" I feel really sorry for disturbing him this early for reasons that are not important to him.

"Don't be sorry, you didn't wake me up," he replies.

"Did you see Pablo tonight?" I ask him desperately.

"Not today." He answers shortly and then asks, "He told me you guys were separated the last time I saw him. Is it true?"

"No, we are not. Who told you that?" I ask in surprise.

"He did. He was with a girl, maybe he didn't want me to ask him questions."

"A girl? Do we know her?"

"You will have to ask Pablo for that. I am sorry." He says with a low voice, like he didn't want to hurt me more. "How are you doing? Are you okay, Cia?"

"I don't know, maybe I am. I have no idea, thank you Jordan."

"Any time, Cia, if you need someone to talk to, know I am here for you, sweetheart."

"Yes, thank you."

"Good night, take care," he finished, then ended the call.

Jordan is always so nice to me, and I feel bad sometimes that I didn't even realize he liked me that way. I said yes to Pablo. I am not sure if I would say yes to him. Jordan is way out of my league. He is so cute, well, Pablo is cute too, but Jordan… apart from being handsome, he comes from a very influential family; his father is a college football coach, and he used to play football himself before. His mother is a retired model, but she still models sometimes. Even Jordan has been in a few commercials since he was young. That is all apart from the fact that he was famous in school; every girl wanted to be with him. His father is a mix of black American and German, while his mother is white. He is tall and masculine, and I really never thought he had a thing for me, out of all the girls who throw themselves at him.

I fell asleep eventually, and when I woke up, Pablo was still not home. I called him one more time, but he didn't pick up. I decide to call his mother without telling her the truth, just to see if he is at her house. She says he was not there and promises to call him and get back to me. I take a shower and feed the baby, thanking God that I have the calmest baby in the whole world. He eats, sleeps, and only cries when he is hungry.

I find a text from Pablo when I check my phone: 'Stop telling my mother our business, I will be home later.' I already feel angry at him; if he doesn't want to be married anymore, he better tell me. All I know is I am not ready to share him with anyone.

My phone rings and brings me back from my thoughts. It is Pablo's mother. "Don't worry, Pablo is at Valeria's house; she needed help."

"Valeria?" I ask.

"Yes, my friend Naomi's sister. You know her." She says, and I remember her, even her voice. She is the V who called yesterday.

"Yes, I know her, thank you, Mama," I say.

"He is okay; call me if you need anything, darling."

"Thank you."

Pablo's mother is so lovely, she helps me with the baby all the time, and it helps that she is a housewife.

That woman…Valeria, I know her very well. Her sister, Aunt Naomi, is best friends with Pablo's mother. Valeria is twenty-eight years old, almost ten years older than us. I remember Pablo telling me she used to babysit them when they were little. It can't be her, but what if it is? I know there is only one way to understand this. I know where she lives, I remember that on my wedding, her house was used for my preparation because she lives ten minutes from Pablo's parents' house, where our ceremony was held.

I put on sweatpants, a t-shirt, plus a hoodie. I fed Antonio first before I called for an Uber. It takes my son and me straight to Valeria's apartment. I knocked twice before the door opened. Standing in front of me is a shirtless Pablo, only wearing a pair of shorts that are not tied well around his waist, so I could see his boxers. I push the door and enter.

"P, wait for me, don't start eating." There goes the nicknames… telling me this is the V from that phone call. She is inside one of the rooms or the toilet, I don't care. What shocks me the most is the scene in front of me.

The sitting room smells like sex; I can smell Pablo's sperm clearly. The pillows are scattered on the ground; the couch has moved a little. Their clothes are scattered everywhere, I can see her dress, his shirt, and pants, and their shoes. It seems they either left their clothes here and did it in bed last night, or they came back and did it in the sitting room because their clothes appear to have been taken off all the way to a door; they trail that way.

"What is going on here? Is she the woman you are cheating me with?" I ask Pablo, who is standing near the door, in shock that I am here. In that moment, the famous Valeria comes out and meets my gaze in surprise. I know she never expected me to be here. She is wearing short, tight shorts with a bra. She looks so beautiful, she is skinnier compared to me, you can tell she exercises, and I have never exercised in my life. Her breasts are two sizes smaller than mine; I am a double D now, while she is maybe a B, and we both know size B is the perfect size of breast a woman can have. She has a flat stomach, of course, because she hadn't had a baby a few months ago. She is Hispanic, which I am not. She is everything I am not. Not to mention that she is older than I, which means she must be good in bed. Fuck me I am going crazy right now.

"Cia, you shouldn't be here. I told you I'm coming back." Pablo says while picking up his clothes and putting them on one by one. Valeria sits on one of the chairs in the dining room unbothered, like she doesn't care what is happening here.

I look at Pablo. "Please tell me this is not happening, Pablo." I cry, wishing it's all a dream.

"You can believe what you want to believe, let's go home," he says, pulling me out, and he is carrying the car seat. I look at Valeria one more time, then I say, "Leave my husband alone, you home wrecker."

She smiles, then says the last thing I expected her to say," There is no home to wreck, darling, just get out of my house." She stands up and locks the door behind us.

Pablo put the baby seat inside the car, I got in the passenger seat, and he drove us home in silence.

"Pablo, I don't want you to see that woman or any other woman," I say desperately. I can't lose Pablo. We have a kid together, but I know the woman is fine; if I don't play my cards well, she will take him away. We reach our house and go inside.

I pull Pablo and kiss him, I can taste her smell on him, and I let him go. "Why don't you go and take a shower, please?" He didn't say anything; he went straight to the bathroom and shower.

He come out on a towel, "Cia, I know I fucked up but can we not tell anyone about this, especially not my mother."

I smile, knowing that this is precisely what I need to keep my husband.

"I won't tell, and I can try to forget about it if you break things with her. Text her now and tell her it's over, that you love me, your wife." I hand him his phone. He took it, texted her, declared his love for me, and said that we are going to try fixing our relationship. I smile but was cut off by a text from her saying 'Bull shit.'

"Block her?" I am angry. I hate this woman so much right now. "And delete all her messages." Pablo goes ahead and does as I say. I smile, feeling like the luckiest girl alive.

I kiss him passionately, and he kisses me back. I love this man, and he is my man. I am not going to let any other woman have him; I know we can get past this. I drop the towel around Pablo's waist and I smile at the view his cock gives. The fact that he is turned on right now, I know we can make it through anything going forward.

I let him go and take off my clothes and jump on the bed, and Pablo follows me. We look at each other as he finds his way inside my pussy. "Mmmmh," I give out a long moan, it has been so long since we had sex, maybe a few weeks, and I miss him so much. He kisses my neck and whispers in my ear, "You feel so good, my love." Hearing Pablo say that to me felt like a dream. These days, we don't often talk during sex, or even when we're just together.

"I love you, Pablo," I whisper in his ear.

"I love you too," he answers while he continues to move in and out of me. We both come so hard in a few minutes.

The next day, I wake up and find the baby is already bathed and changed, also Pablo makes breakfast for me in bed and makes me feel like a Queen, his Queen.

I don't work on weekends, so we'll spend this Sunday chilling at home. We watch movies then have more sex on the bed, in the bathroom, the couch. Pablo finally smiles, and for a perfect day, we are back behaving like the husband and wife we should have been before all this.

Two weeks passed from that day; we never talked about it. It is as if it never happened. Pablo comes back home on time; he didn't go out the past two weekends, which makes me so happy. Also, our sex life is fantastic; we have had more sex in the past two weeks than at any time since we have been together. His papers for his enrollment in the army come, and it's official, he will be leaving in one month.

We agree that I will move in with my mother for the time being, and then we will find a new apartment when he comes back.

Today is Monday, and I am going to the hospital for my son's and my checkup. It's the three-month checkup for him. I scheduled them on the same day, and surprisingly, I was able to get the same day, but I will have to wait for one and a half hours. Pablo went to work, but he will be here to pick us up.

Antonio's checkup went well, and everything is fine with him. When it is my turn, the doctor checks me and then she asks, "Have you got your period post giving birth?

"No! Is it not normal? I asked my mother a few weeks ago, she said it was normal; she didn't get her period until she stopped breastfeeding."

"No, it's normal, but let me check something." She gets the ultrasound and starts looking into my stomach using the small remote for it. I begin to hear the monitor making noise. "What is that, Doctor?"

"It's a heartbeat, you are having another baby."

My God, not again, all this time I did not worry about preventing pregnancy because I didn't get my period, now what am I going to do? Am having another baby fuck me, this is crazy. People usually make mistakes once, not twice. Not that my kids are mistakes, but my having unplanned pregnancies is not fun anymore. All this time, I was so worried about keeping Pablo instead of preventing pregnancy. What am I going to do now? I am going to have two kids by the age of twenty. This is crazy.

Pablo comes and picks us up. We stop by for a cheeseburger and drive home. I'm going to take a shower.

"I'll pick a movie, let's watch something," Pablo says, sitting on the couch.

"Pablo, I need us to talk first," I say, fidgeting with my fingers.

"What's wrong?" Pablo asks me.

"Pablo, I am pregnant," I say. Pablo smiled at first, and then he laughed.

"No! Tell me you're joking!" he says.

"I am not," I answer, looking at him seriously.

"I'm done," he says, walking to the bedroom.

"What do you mean you are done?"

"I mean, I'm done, Cia, with you and this pregnancy of yours that keeps me trapped to you," he yells at me.

"Trapped?" I ask in surprise.

"Yes! Since you got pregnant with Antonio, my life hasn't been the same; all my dreams died. We had to stay in this farce of a marriage for what? I am not happy, my life is miserable, and now you say you are pregnant again. What do you want now for me not to go to the military?"

I am genuinely shocked and hurt by everything Pablo is saying. "Pablo, we got married because we love each other," I say with my eyes full of tears.

"What love? Our parents forced us to get married; I would have never married you if it were up to me." His words cut my heart into little pieces. "Just know I am going to follow my heart and my dreams, you stay here, keep getting pregnant. I am done, whatever this was, it's over. I am done being miserable." He picked up his keys and left.

I sit down and cry, not believing what just happened. Pablo says he never loved me and has been miserable. Calling our marriage a false... I can't think, maybe I am having a nightmare. I really need someone to wake me up.

After like two hours, I started to call Pablo. A few calls later, he switched off his phone. I cried so hard that night until I fell asleep. The following day, I called my boss to excuse myself from going to work for the next couple of days. There is no way I can function at work like this. I try Pablo's phone again, it's still off, or maybe he blocked me.

It is two in the afternoon, and Pablo is nowhere. I know he might be with his mother, but when I called his mother, she did not say anything, like she knew nothing. In fact, she asked for Pablo, which meant he hadn't talked to her in a few days. Yeah, Pablo is like that with his mother; they will text every day, but talk a few days a week. I talk to my mother every day. She actually called in the morning, and I told her everything was okay. I hate lying to her, but I can't say anything till I talk to Pablo. I call him again, but his phone is still off. At this point, I am so mad and heartbroken. I decided to do the last thing I should do.

I called Jordan to ask him for a favor. I'm not really sure if he will grant it to me.

"Hallo!" His voice is so deep and heavy, he sounds really grown, and it's so sexy.

"Hi! Jordan, I have a request. I am sorry; it's okay if you can't do it. I will understand." I say quickly, hopefully I don't talk myself out of it.

"Well, you already know I'm here for you, Cia. Ask me anything, sweetheart." He replies. Suddenly, I felt confident with his answer.

"A little bird told me that you like me, but maybe you just used to," I said, trying to lighten the mood as I made my request.

"It's probably true, sweetheart," he replied, and a brief silence hung between us as we absorbed the weight of his words. When I didn't respond, he asked, "So, what do you need from me?"

"Can you take me anywhere you can, and please make me forget him?" I say it finally; I really need to forget Pablo in any way possible.

"Is everything okay? Are you okay, CIA?" He asks, and I can hear his confusion.

"I need to forget him, please help me," I say in a lower voice, like a whisper, not wanting to cry again.

"I will pick you up at five pm," he says.

"Thank you." I hang up, not wanting to know where we are going or what we are going to do. I will let myself be free and let Jordan do anything he wants with me, because I'm tired of everything that's happening in my life.

I went to the bathroom and did some cleaning up on my body. I texted him to meet me at the back street of Pablo's house, because I need to take the baby to his mother. I know I can't take him to my mother, she will see through my eyes that I am not okay.

I wear a short black dress with heels; I tie my hair in a low-back ponytail. I applied a little makeup to bring out my natural skin's shine a little.

Pablo's mother didn't ask any questions, I just said that I'm going out with some friends. She knows I'm young and free to do what I want. She misses Antonio, so she was more than happy to babysit him.

I had walked a few feet when a car drove near me; inside was Jordan. I smiled and got in the car, and he leaned in to help me with the seatbelt. He strapped it carefully and attentively—it was so sexy. His face was so close to mine; he was incredibly handsome.

I had no idea he liked me when Pablo started asking me out; I thought he was out of my league. He had been the school's best quarterback, with all the girls wanting to be with him. Women basically threw themselves at him. I didn't know what I would have done if I had known back then that he liked me. I still didn't believe he had any feelings for me. What if it was all a lie?

"How are you?" he asked, already driving and looking straight at the road.

I looked at him again, then turned to gaze outside. He placed his hand on my bare thighs, as the dress I wore covered only a few parts of my upper thighs.

"Cia, what happened? Are things really over with him?" he asked again, and I knew I had to say something. This guy had left whatever he was doing in his busy schedule, and he was here taking me somewhere—I didn't know where. All so I could forget my troubles.

"Yeah! It's over," I replied as he massaged my left thigh with his big hand in silence for a few minutes.

Yes, minutes—and it felt like heaven. It turned me on. I wasn't sure why, but being in that car with Jordan made me feel a different type of energy.

"How have you been?" I asked, trying to distract myself from whatever I was feeling.

He took his hand off my skin, and I felt a loneliness I had never felt before. It was as if my skin had known his touch before he had even touched me.

"I have been great. School and football are all good. Actually, my coach thinks I'm doing so good I can graduate early, so I don't have to wait four years to be drafted."

"Wow! That's amazing, I am so happy for you."

I didn't tell him what I felt on the inside. His parents must be so happy and proud of him. I think I have disappointed my mother a lot; I have no idea what she will say if I tell her I'm pregnant again.

"Thank you," he said, looking at me. Our eyes met for a few seconds, then he turned back to the road.

I had no idea where we were going.

"You know, I still can't believe you are here with me."

He smiled. "I hope you don't wake me if it's a dream."

We both laughed at that. It was crazy. While I had been busy struggling with Pablo, here was this wonderful, handsome man hoping for a dream of me.

We stayed quiet for the rest of the ride downtown. I looked outside as I recognized some of the buildings. I hadn't been in this side of town for a while. With my life being so busy with the baby, it had been a minute.

We stopped at a very beautiful hotel.

"Wait here," he said as he got out of the car.

I saw him give the valet the keys, then he walked to my side and opened the door for me. I got out and followed him, holding his hand. We arrived at the reception, where he provided his information, and the receptionist handed him a key. He led us to the elevator with our hands entwined.

We entered the room. It was big and nice—actually beautiful. There was a large king-size bed, a small table with chairs around it, and a double sofa on the side.

"I need to use the restroom," I said.

I knew what would happen in that room, and I was ready for it. That's why I had asked him for help. But I couldn't calm my nerves.

I entered the restroom and looked at myself to make sure everything was okay. I peed quickly and cleaned myself with the wipes I had. I sprayed myself a little so I would smell fresh before going out.

Jordan was sitting on the couch when I got out of the bathroom. He had taken off his shirt—he wore an undershirt—and he had also taken off his shoes. I stood next to the bed, looking at him. He turned his head to me and caught me checking him out. He smiled and stood up quickly.

He put one of his hands on my waist and used his free hand to hold the side of my neck, resting his thumb on my jawline. I turned my eyes and looked at him. He was so handsome, his eyes looking at me with so much desire. We locked eyes for a few seconds, then he asked me, "Are you okay with this? I'm not going to hold it against you if you change your mind."

"I am okay."

With my permission, he moved forward and closed the gap between our mouths. At first, it was a closed kiss, and then he opened his mouth and deepened the kiss, sliding his tongue inside my mouth, searching for my tongue. He moved his hand to the back of my head, holding me closer. I put one of my hands on his chest, feeling the hard surface through the fabric of his t-shirt, and the other hand rested behind his head, a little down near his neck.

The kiss was long and deep—so passionate, it made me wetter than I already was. I was so wet, like I had already come. Could someone orgasm just by being kissed? I had no idea. I guessed I had more to discover about life.

He bit my lower lip a little as he broke the kiss, and we were both gasping for air. The room felt so hot; I felt like I was sweating, but I wasn't. I looked at him, and we were both blushing. He gave me one more kiss and sat me down on the bed.

Jordan knelt down between my legs, and I reached out and kissed him again. When we let go, he held one of my legs and started kissing it from the thigh down to my toes. He took off my shoe. He massaged my foot, then slid my big toe into his mouth, sucking it like a lollipop. I felt shots of electricity all the way to my head.

"Mmmh!" I moaned so loud.

He did the same thing to my other leg.

He moved his hands onto my ass under the dress while still kneeling between my legs. He gave my ass a little squeeze, laying his head on my boobs. Jordan pushed my dress above my waist, then pulled my panties off.

I looked at him as he took his hand with my panties in it and smelled it for a few seconds, his eyes closed. I watched him, fascinated. Jordan held my waist with one hand while sliding the other between my legs, massaging my clit for a while before sliding two fingers inside my pussy and starting to finger fuck me so hard. I screamed with pleasure, holding on to his head, which was buried on my stomach, kissing me.

I came so hard—his fingers felt so good.

He stood up and pulled the dress off of me, along with my bra.

"Move back," he said in a lower voice with authority. Like a good girl, I moved back to the middle of the bed.

Jordan took off his t-shirt and unbuttoned his belt. Our eyes locked as he climbed onto the bed and hovered over me, covering my mouth with his, and we kissed passionately.

When he let go of my lips, he moved to my neck, then to my shoulders, leaving traces of wet kisses. He slid down to my breast; my nipple was hard. He pinched each of my nipples one after the other, carefully—not squeezing too hard, I was sure, because he knew I was breastfeeding. My body was on fire. I couldn't even voice a word when I felt his mouth on one of my breasts, sucking on my nipple. I was sure he sucked and swallowed some milk in the process, but he didn't seem to care.

I moaned so loud—his lips felt so good on my nipples, all I could do was bury my fingers in his hair. As if that wasn't enough, Jordan slid farther down, kissing my stomach, then sucking on my belly button for a moment before he spread my thighs with his hands and buried his mouth on my clit, eating me up.

"Oooh! My God, aaaaaaaaaaaah!" I screamed with pleasure; my whole body was electrified. I gripped the pillow with my fingers, trying to close my legs, but his hold was so tight, and he kept his mouth there, unbothered.

I had multiple orgasms; my whole body was shaking by the time he let me go.

Before I could come down from the high I was on, he hovered on top of me, and I could feel the head of his penis pressing against my pussy entrance so hard. I hadn't seen his penis, but I could feel it. My eyes were closed.

"Cia, open your eyes," he whispered in my ear.

I opened my eyes, looking right at him. He bit his lower lip, then pushed himself inside of me. I was so wet, but his big penis made me feel too tight. I screamed with pressure as he pushed in again, burying his whole length inside me, and my eyes closed automatically. He was bigger than Pablo—way bigger—and he felt way better.

He kept thrusting slowly in and out, kissing me on the lips, my neck, and the upper side of my breast. Then he knelt on the bed with his knees, sliding me between his thighs. He held my legs at the thighs, pressing my feet to each side of his shoulders as he thrust in and out of my pussy, increasing the friction as he kept going.

At this point, I didn't even remember my name. The level of intimacy I felt right then—I had never experienced anything like it before.

After a few—I didn't know—minutes or seconds, I didn't care. Jordan turned me around onto my stomach so I was giving him my back. He tried to make me stand on my knees, but I ended up lying in a child's pose by the time he pushed himself inside me again. So, he decided to put some pillows under my thighs to elevate my ass a little, then he slid inside me. He felt so good. He kissed my back, my neck, and before I realized it, he whispered the last words I expected to hear.

"I love you, Leoncia."

I heard him loud and clear, but I was feeling so high at that moment, so I turned my head and kissed him like my life depended on it.

We turned again, my back on the bed and him on top of me—only this time, he pulled my left leg with his arm up to my stomach, and his other hand crossed under my back, pulling me closer as he plunged in and out with equal, quick pace until he exploded inside me like a volcano. I shuddered with my fifth—or maybe more—orgasm. I had lost count of how many times I had come so far.

He kissed me so passionately before letting go and disappearing into the restroom. I stayed in bed with my eyes closed; my body was struggling to regain its strength.

Jordan came back holding two towels—one was wet with warm water—and he placed it on my pussy, gently cleaning me up. He went back to the restroom and returned with the same towels, this time cleaning my whole body. He was sponge bathing me. Then he dried me off. He pulled the blanket over me so I wouldn't feel cold, then jumped on the bed and lay next to me. We were sleeping on our sides, facing each other. I looked at him, and a tear escaped my eye.

"What's wrong, love? Why are you crying?" he asked, wiping the tears off my cheeks. "Did I hurt you?" He seemed worried.

"No! I am okay. Actually, I'm more than okay. Thank you, Jordan," I said, and he smiled.

"Why?" he asked.

"I asked you to make me forget him. Well, I see you ended up erasing him from every inch of my body. Now, how am I going to forget this night?" I asked, smiling—because it was true. Jordan had just made a new mark on me. This was more than I expected, more than my wildest dream.

"That was the plan," he said so calmly.

"So! You had a plan?" I asked, laughing.

"Maybe. Are you hungry?"

"I am starving," I answered. Who wouldn't be hungry after all that?

"Okay! I'll order room service," he said, moving to the phone. "What do you want to eat?"

"I'll eat anything with wings."

One hour later, our food arrived, and we set everything on the bed. I wore my bra and panties, and he was in his boxers. He ordered wings and fries for me, while he had a cheeseburger. He fed me a few times, and I liked that.

We moved to the couch after we finished eating. He wanted us to watch a movie. I sat on his lap as soon as he sat down. We started kissing again, and within a few minutes, I could feel him getting hard. I slid off and knelt in front of him, took out his penis, and put it in my mouth. This man had given me the best time of my life—I was going to use my experience and return the favor. I sucked on his penis head like a lollipop, the way Pablo used to teach me.

A few minutes later, Jordan and I had another hot round of sex on the couch, finishing off on the bed with him on top of me, my legs spread open on both sides of his waist.

By the time we were done, it was almost one a.m. "I have to go," I whispered in his ear as we cuddled under the covers.

"I know," he said sadly.

"We can take a shower together," I said, trying to lighten the moment.

"I don't want to wash you off of me yet," he said—and my heart melted. How come he was so perfect while I was so imperfect in so many ways? I smiled and went to shower. There was no way I was going to pick up my son smelling like sex—well, hot sex.

My God. What was this? What was I going to do now? This man had completely swept me off my feet, and this was by far the best night of my life. But back to reality—my marriage was over, while there was a baby inside my tummy. My life was so messy, and I had no idea what I was doing. The man in the next room told me he loved me, while my husband—the father of my kids—declared he never loved me. That's why it was so hard to believe Jordan really loved me. What if I was just one of his many women? What he did to me today, maybe he had done the same to all the girls who had him before. I couldn't really blame them for throwing themselves at him. I basically did that too. But the guy was so good, he was making me rethink my whole relationship with Pablo. It was like all this time, we had been wasting our time on each other.

He was fully dressed when I got out. I didn't think he was serious. "So you're seriously not going to take a shower?" I asked, surprised.

He smiled and said, "Not yet. It's not every day I get this chance to have your smell all over me." He said, "Kiss me."

I let go as soon as I felt the heat between us start to form again. I opened my purse and took out my phone. There were a lot of missed calls—from my mother, Pablo's mother, and Pablo. I opened the texts and found five: two from my mother asking where I was and telling me to call her. The other two were from Pablo, demanding that I get home as soon as possible from wherever I was. One more text came from

Pablo's mother, saying Pablo had already taken the baby home two hours ago.

"I need to call my mother," I said to him. He moved to the bed, giving me space, and staying busy with his phone.

"Hello!" I said when my mother picked up. I knew she must have been asleep.

"Hi! Mama, I am sorry, are you sleeping?"

"No! Where are you? You had all of us worried. Pablo is looking for you."

"Why? I told his mother I was going out with my friends."

"Who? I don't know any friend of yours. You don't even go out nowadays," she said, surprised.

"I know, and I will explain later, Mama. I have to go."

I sent a thank-you text to Pablo's mother and put the phone back in my bag.

"Are you ready?" Jordan asked me.

"Yes!" I answered, looking at him.

"I'm not going to ask you when I'll see you again. But I need you to know, I will always be here for you," he said, then kissed my cheek.

"I know, thank you so much, Jordan," I said, smiling because I was genuinely grateful that he gave me the best night of my life. He put his hand on my back, to the side of my waist, and we walked out of the hotel together.

The valet brought the car for us. Jordan opened the door for me, then got in on the driver's side and started driving to my house. I gave him the address. He played his music playlist—the songs he said he loved. He held my hand the whole way home.

"We are here," he announced as we stopped in front of my apartment. "Wait, please," he said like it was painful for him to drop me off. And I think it was. I wished I didn't have to come back, if it weren't for my child.

"Jordan!" I called him. He was hiding his eyes from mine. I pulled his face up, and I could see his eyes were getting watery. "I can't promise you anything right now. My life is a mess."

"I know," he answered, and then we kissed one more time. He got out and opened the door for me. We hugged each other tightly, then he kissed me on the cheek.

"You'll call me, right?" he asked. And I understood exactly what he wanted—a chance for us to be together. But I wasn't sure that was possible right now. I just nodded yes and opened the door to my apartment while he got back into his car and drove away.

I locked the door and took off my shoes. When I turned around, Pablo was sitting on the couch.

"So, you were with Jordan?" he asked, standing, angry.

"Yes! I was," I said, walking to the bedroom.

Pablo grabbed my hand, and I pulled away.

"What were you doing with him?" he asked, looking straight at my face.

"Fucking," I said bluntly.

"What the fuck?" he asked, shocked.

"I just had sex with Jordan. The best I've... No! No! It was the most amazing sex I've ever had in my life," I said, smiling.

Pablo raised his hand and slapped me so hard. I raised my hand and slapped him back.

He started laughing, and I could see how mad he was. I took a few steps back.

"How does it feel to know it's not only you who can sleep around?" I said angrily.

He laughed more, clapping his hands. "I never thought you were this stupid. Jordan goes through women like clothes—you should know that. He has women throw themselves at him. What? You think you'll be anything more than one of his many other women? If he really loves you, why do you think he never made any effort back then to keep you? Now that you're fat and ugly with almost two kids, you think he's going to waste his time with you?"

"Stop, Pablo," I said, crying. "Stop talking."

"Why? Because you know it's the truth? Let me tell you, no one will ever be stupid enough to be with someone like you. I know better now, after you destroyed my life. I didn't even love you. I was only forced to be with you out of my good heart. Wait a minute, is that baby Jordan's?"

"No! The baby is yours, unfortunately," I said, tears in my eyes.

"I'll do a DNA test to make sure. I don't believe anything coming from that mouth anymore. I'm leaving. Whatever we had is over now," he said, then grabbed his keys and left.

I sat on the couch crying so hard.

After some time, I changed and fell asleep. In the morning, I was woken by a phone call from Pablo's mother.

"Hello!" I picked up.

"Cia, what is going on? Pablo said you guys are divorcing. Is it true you cheated on him?" she asked.

"He said I cheated?" I asked, not shocked. At this point, he was playing the victim.

"Didn't he tell you he's the one who started all this, cheating on me with Aunt Valeria?"

"Valeria? My Valeria?" she asked, shocked.

"Yes! Your son is having sex with Valeria."

Then I hung up.

Chapter V:
Moving On

I checked my phone and saw a text from Jordan: *"Good morning, beautiful. How are you?"* I didn't answer; I didn't know what to tell him. I knew what happened between us was real and amazing, but my life at that moment was not ready for him. I couldn't jump into another relationship, much less with him. Pablo had a point. There was no way Jordan would want to be with me with all the baggage I had.

I took a shower and changed. Then I called my mother and asked her to pick me up. My phone started blowing up with texts and calls from Pablo, and I ignored him, knowing the story of him and Valeria having sex was heating up. He texted to curse me out for destroying his life. I didn't care; he destroyed mine. Knowing that he never loved me made it all worse.

My mother came one hour later. I had already showered and packed some clothes for me and Antonio. I didn't want to stay in that place any second longer. I also took the groceries I had in the refrigerator. I was going to stay with my mother.

I got a message from Jordan as soon as we got to my mother's house, after I had ignored his calls. "I am outside your apartment. Can I see you? Pablo called me, saying I broke your marriage. I thought you two were not a thing anymore." I knew Pablo would try to contact him.

I decided to call him. I stepped outside before he picked up.

"Hello! Cia, you okay?" he asked, sounding worried.

"I am okay, but I am not there, Jordan," I said, really wishing I could see him. His hug was so warm; I bet it would keep me warm a little.

"Where are you? Can I see you, love?" He said that word again. I didn't want to believe it, even if it was used as a nickname.

"I can't see you, Jordan. I'm sorry. We cannot be together," I said, tears coming down like waterfalls from my eyes. I didn't think I still had more tears left after I cried for the rest of that morning.

"Cia, please don't give up on us yet. I know it's soon for you to start a new relationship, but I can wait. I will wait for you. But don't push me out of your life." He sounded so serious, like he meant every word he said.

"Jordan, I am pregnant." I left that word hanging there. I hadn't said it to anyone else besides Pablo. "And it's not yours. I think it's best that we stay friends. I am so sorry."

He stayed quiet for a while. For a second, I thought he had hung up.

"Yeah! Let's be friends. Leoncia, just know I am always here for you, just one phone call away."

"Thank you."

With that, he ended the call, and I realized right then and there I had just lost the best man in my life.

I went back inside. My mother was changing Antonio. I sat next to her. I decided I was going to tell my mother everything. She was my only person—the only person I knew who would hold my hand in any situation without judging me.

My mother hugged me after I finished telling her how my marriage died.

"Listen, a marriage is not a one-person work or responsibility. It takes two people and a lot of things put together for it to survive. It is unfortunate you had to go through this at your age. But life needs to go on always. So I need you to grow a pair and get strong for your kids."

Two weeks later, Pablo left for the military. We were not talking. I thought he blocked my number, and I didn't care— I would not want to see him either. His mother came to pick up Antonio so he could say goodbye to him and drop him back later. That's how I found out he was leaving.

Jordan and I kept in contact. He called me at first every week, then a couple of days a week, and now almost every day. I now knew his schedule by heart. We had become pretty close by the time I gave birth to my baby girl.

Yes, I had a baby girl. I called her Liliana. I say *I called* her because Pablo did not want to get involved with her at all. When she was born, he came because his mother asked me to call her when I was in labor, which I did.

When he got to the hospital, Jordan was there too, and he was so angry that he ordered a DNA test. That pissed me off, and I did not put him on the birth certificate. When the DNA results showed that he was the father, Pablo unblocked me and started telling me I should put his name on the certificate. I told him to do it himself, which he did, and I took my sweet time to sign the papers. By then, we were already divorced.

A few months after I gave birth, on my birthday in July, my aunt decided to throw me a party. I wasn't prepared for anything. It was at a karaoke pub, because I was turning twenty-one—finally old enough to go out drinking legally. Jordan couldn't come because of his busy schedule. His coach wanted him to graduate from college by December since there was a big chance he would be drafted into the NFL next year. He sent his sister Juliana with a gift.

When I was pregnant, Jordan taught me how to drive. Yes, I didn't know how to drive before. Then I took an online driving course, and after that, I got my license. But I was still sharing a car with my mother.

The birthday party was amazing. I laughed so hard. Everyone picked a song and sang—it was hilarious, especially because none of us could actually sing. It was refreshing to let go of motherhood just for once. My life has been all about my kids lately, especially now that they only have me to rely on, since their father is nowhere to be found. I don't even know where he was assigned after finishing his military training.

When it came time for gifts, everyone gave me something. Then Juliana stood up to deliver Jordan's surprise.

"Attention," Juliana said, clicking her wine glass. "So, Cia, I have a gift from Jordan." Everyone giggled. Almost everyone there knew Jordan, and they all suspected there was something more than friendship between us—if I would just let it happen.

"I guess Santa came early for you," she added, holding out a car key.

Yes, a car. Jordan bought me a car.

"No! He didn't?" I asked, completely shocked.

Two months ago, when Jordan came to town for Juliana's high school graduation, he went with me to a few car lots. I had been looking for a car, and I found a Honda that I really liked. But my credit score was bad. It had been messed up ever since Pablo left me with credit card debt. I don't know what he told his parents after he left, but they stopped helping me with anything related to the kids. And I was too proud to beg. His mother still kept in touch, just so she could see the kids—but that was it.

Because of my credit, I couldn't get any reasonable offers. Jordan offered to co-own the car with me, but I declined. So today, he sent his sister with the key.

"He wants you to call him so he can give you all the details," Juliana said, handing me the car key. "Happy birthday to you." She smiled. Well, Juliana is our number-one fan—she even said she wanted to witness our love story in real life and open a group chat of us three.

Jordan has started making extra money from TV commercials—he's that good at football. His parents also still cover his expenses; his dad deposits money into his account every month.

"Hello!" Jordan's voice is getting deeper as he gets older. It's so sexy. I don't know what tomorrow will bring, or if we'll ever be together, but I love what we have. Our friendship is one of a kind.

"Hi! Thank you for the gift. You know you didn't have to," I said, smiling. This man has done so much for me without expecting anything in return. I know all it would take is one word, and he'd be mine. But I also know better than to drag him into my messy life. It wouldn't be fair. That's why I've kept us as friends—it's better that way.

"I know, but I wanted to spoil you a little, sweetheart. Happy birthday," he said, making me blush. He always makes me feel so special.

"Thank you. You really did spoil me, and I appreciate it so much."

"You're welcome," he said, and then sent me the details of the car shop. Apparently, I'd need to go sign the title—he had already paid for it in full and put my name on it.

I don't know how I got so lucky to have someone like him in my life. For the past year and a half, since Jordan came into my world, things have truly been better. He helps me financially without me ever asking. He's the first person I talk to about anything—well, after my mother, of course. And he always listens. He always does something.

Juliana came with me the next day to pick up the car. I still can't believe it—I actually have a car.

Jordan was able to finish his finals before the football season started. I went to a couple of his games—some with his family and some alone. His team made it to the finals. We all went, except my mother, who always volunteered to stay with the kids. Even my aunt came. Jordan's team won, and he also took home two medals. It was amazing.

A week later, his parents threw a party, and Jordan showed up with a girl named Hanna. She was Filipino, younger than me, and absolutely beautiful. He introduced her as his girlfriend, and my heart broke into so many pieces. I couldn't blame him—it had been almost two years since we had that unforgettable night together. I still felt turned on whenever I thought of it. Maybe I just needed a reality check—how it felt to lose the hope of ever being with him again.

"This is bad. Jordan, where did you get this girl?" Juliana typed in the group chat that night.

"What's wrong with you, July? Stop, " Jordan replied.

I stayed out of the conversation.

"I'm dropping this group. I thought you guys were strong enough to fight for each other."

That was July's last message. Jordan and I said nothing. Two hours later, she dissolved the group and called me.

"Cia, you're really not going to fight for him?" she asked.

"July, he's not mine to fight for, and he can date whoever he wants. Besides, the girl is gorgeous. I don't think I stand a chance," I said.

"Well, I hate her. Because I know Jordan loves you and not her," she insisted.

"He *used to* love me. And he's free to date whoever he wants. It's okay," I replied, even though I knew it wasn't. But what could I do? I had no control over any of it.

"Okay. I hope he gets his senses back." July hung up, leaving me with a flood of thoughts.

I really hoped he wasn't dating anyone—at least, not anyone *but me*. But it was out of my hands, and Jordan had every right to move on.

We kept our friendship, even while he dated Hanna, but it wasn't the same. I wasn't as free to call him anymore. I thought twice before texting. The little movie nights and shopping dates we used to share came to an end. I missed him terribly. And I swear, if there was even the smallest chance for us to be together again, I'd jump without hesitation. But maybe I had already lost him for good.

Three months passed. Today was the day Jordan was going to be drafted. His mother, Mrs. Franklin, prepared a small gathering at their home with friends and family to celebrate and be there when he received the call. Juliana invited me.

At first, I didn't want to go. I hadn't talked to or seen Jordan in a month and a half. But it was his big day—and we were still friends. We still texted, even if less often.

I wore a black short skirt with a gray T-shirt tied at the back, leaving a small part of my waist exposed. I had lost a lot of weight since giving birth to my baby girl. Still, my boobs and ass were big enough, though I'd dropped bra sizes. I knew Hanna, being thinner, would probably look better in Jordan's eyes. To say I was jealous of her was an understatement. I should've been the one with Jordan, but I knew I'd blown my chance.

The housekeeper opened the door and directed me to the sitting room, where everyone was gathered. Jordan saw me first. He jumped up from the couch, where he'd been sitting beside Hanna, and came to hug me.

I hugged him back, closing my eyes. My arms wrapped around his shoulders and down to his back as I buried my nose into his neck, inhaling his scent. I missed him so much. His big hands held me around my waist. I could feel his face on my neck too, doing the same—breathing me in. We stood like that, hugging, for I don't even know how long, eyes closed.

"Hi!" Hanna said behind him.

He let go of me quickly. She grabbed his hand and pulled him back toward her.

"Hi, Hanna," I greeted her, my eyes lingering on Jordan, who was looking right back at me. He wore blue jeans and a black hoodie. She wore a short, tight pink dress that looked great on her.

"What's your name again? Tia?" she asked, mispronouncing my name.

Jordan turned and looked at her in shock, as if to say she *should* have known it.

"Her name is Leoncia," Jordan said, making me look at him. The way he says my name is so sexy—it turns me on every time. I love how his gorgeous lips move as he pronounces it.

"My friends call me Cia," I added, just as Juliana joined us.

"Cia! You made it. Come, I have a gift for Liliana," July said, pulling me away from them. Thank God—things were starting to get awkward. July is obsessed with my daughter, Liliana. She always spoils her with gifts.

"Another gift? You know the girl is getting spoiled with these gifts," I said, smiling.

"Let her be, as long as I'm her favorite auntie." We both laughed while she handed me the gift.

Friends and family kept arriving, and eventually the food was served. Jordan and I didn't interact again the whole time. Hanna was all over him. We just looked at each other once in a while. That day made me realize how much I truly loved Jordan—and that I lost my chance to be with him. My heart ached. Even though he was never really mine, it still felt like he was snatched away from me.

"Alright, everyone, it's time. I need all of you here on the couch, please," Mrs. Franklin called out, gathering everyone to sit as we waited for Jordan to receive the call.

There was a couch with chairs set behind it, all arranged in front of a backdrop with a banner showing Jordan's picture. His mother went all out preparing for this day. Jordan sat in the middle of the couch. His mother and father sat to his left. On his right were Hanna and Juliana. I sat directly behind the couch, in the middle, right behind Jordan. Other friends and family were seated all around. There were a lot of us.

Before the call began, I leaned forward and placed my hands on Jordan's shoulders. Then I whispered in his left ear,

"I'm so proud of you." He turned around and smiled at me as I let go.

Then the call came. Jordan had been chosen to join the Los Angeles football team. We all clapped and cheered while the cameras captured everything.

He hugged his mother for a few seconds, then turned around, grabbed both my cheeks, and kissed me on the mouth.

I was surprised at first, but when he parted his lips for an open-mouth kiss, I responded the same. I closed my eyes, feeling the kiss deepen. He slid one hand to the back of my head and the other around my waist as he climbed onto the couch, kneeling. I was still sitting on my chair, but only halfway.

The room went quiet for a second.

Then some of his friends started whistling.

Chapter VI:
Priorities

"What's the fuck, Jordan?" Hanna screamed, bringing us back to reality. I tried to let go, knowing we messed up, but Jordan pulled me back and kissed me again. With that, Hanna ran and left.

"Jordan, you are not going to hug your father," Mr. Franklin said, and then Jordan let me go. We both smiled at each other before he got off the couch and hugged his father. I looked at Juliana, who was smiling at me, and I smiled back, surprised by what was happening. I turned to the left and found Jordan's mother glaring at me. I knew she wasn't happy with what just happened. I knew Mrs. Franklin was never a fan of mine.

Everyone congratulated Jordan for a while, then he grabbed my hand and pulled me to him.

"We need to talk, come with me," he said, and I followed him to his room.

I had never been in his room before. We usually didn't hang out at this house, and when I came, it was for special occasions that never ended with me in his room. It was big and nice, with boy vibes. There was a shelving table with footballs and the medals he received from high school to now. As I looked around, Jordan stood and looked at me until I realized he was checking me out.

"What?" I asked shyly.

"You are so beautiful," he said, closing the gap between us, and we started kissing again. This time we were alone, so the kiss got more heated, with his hands traveling from the back of my back to my ass. He squeezed my butt cheeks, making both of us laugh.

"So now can you be my girlfriend?" he asked seductively in my ear while he bit the side of my ear playfully.

"I thought you had a girlfriend," I said, smiling.

"So, I had a girlfriend, yes. Then I saw this beautiful, gorgeous woman who made me forget I had a girlfriend." He smiled.

"I didn't make you do anything. And yes, I will be your girlfriend, Jordan," I said, then kissed him again.

"I am not dreaming, right? You just said yes to be my girlfriend."

"I did. Ooh! My God, Jordan, I am your girlfriend," I said, crushing our lips together again. We kissed until we both needed to gasp for air, but Jordan moved to my neck, kissing it while I held his head. He held one of my breasts, massaging it, and I let out a moan, then realized this was not the right place for what we were doing.

"Jordan, we can't do this here," I said in his ear.

"I know, let's go somewhere else." He nodded in agreement.

"But you need to call Hanna first."

He nodded and took out his phone. I sat on the bed as he dialed her number, putting her on speaker.

"I was wondering if you'd realize I left," she said as she picked up the call.

"Hanna, I'm sorry. I didn't mean to hurt you," Jordan said.

"Well, congratulations, you did just that." Jordan didn't say anything for a few seconds, and Hanna said, "She is the girl you told me about? Your one and only love?"

"Yes," he answered, looking at me, and I smiled, surprised that he talked about me with Hanna.

"Does she love you?" she asked.

"I'm not sure, but I love her," he said, and my heart melted for him right there. I took his free hand and kissed it.

"I hope she is head over heels in love with you. You deserve that, Jordan. I wish I could have made you forget her," she said sadly.

"Trust me, I tried at some point. I wish you all the best, Hanna."

"Well, congratulations." With that, she hung up.

"You told her about me?" I asked, smiling.

"Well, my heart is stubborn. I only love you," he said. I kissed him so passionately, still not believing he was all mine, completely mine.

"And mine loves you too," I said as we pulled out of the kiss. Jordan looked at me, surprised while smiling.

"Did you just say you love me?" he asked.

"Jordan Franklin, I am head over heels in love with you," I said, smiling so hard my cheeks hurt.

"Fuck, that's so sexy. Tell me I'm not dreaming; trust me, I've dreamt this before," he said, and I laughed so hard.

"Well, this is real. It is happening." We kissed again and again and again.

"So, can your mother stay with the kids a little longer? I want to take you somewhere," Jordan said, smiling.

"Let me talk to her," I said, taking my phone out.

I called my mother, and she was happy to stay with the kids, also happy that Jordan and I were together. I talked to my mother about everything, so she knew that I loved Jordan and how much he meant to me.

Jordan opened his laptop and started scrolling through the internet for the best romantic getaway in Galveston. I sat behind him, pressing myself to his back. I crossed one of my hands from his left shoulder to his right shoulder, then placed my other hand on his lower chest above his belly button, under the hoodie he was wearing. Then I started kissing his neck. A moan escaped his lips as I deepened the kiss on his skin.

"Sweetheart, you are not helping," he said, turning to look at me.

"I know. It's just you are so handsome and I'm horny." We both laughed.

"You know I'm already crazy over you. You don't need to drive me crazier." We kissed again and again.

"Okay, I will sit here with my hands closed so you can concentrate," I said, moving to the small couch in his room.

"Good girl, that's a smart move."

We smiled at each other for a second before he shifted his concentration back to the computer. I sat there watching him dreamily.

Twenty minutes later, we had a hotel room booked at one of the best hotels in Galveston and were ready to go.

"We have a problem," I said before we got back to the living room, where everybody was.

"What problem?" Jordan asked, holding my waist, kissing my forehead, then resting his against mine. I laid both of my hands on his chest.

"I don't have clothes to wear. We may need to go back to my house before we go."

"That's not a problem at all. First, you may not need clothes. Second, we can buy some on the way there," he said, smiling.

I smiled back. "Mmmmh! Okay then, problem solved."

We both laughed, and he held my hand as we walked back into the living room.

"Please tell me you guys are together already?" Juliana asked as we entered.

"Well, family, meet my girlfriend," Jordan said, smiling at me. We kissed with closed lips while everyone clapped and laughed, everyone except his mother, who was just quiet.

"I told you, Mama. Give me my hundred bucks," Juliana said to her mother.

"You guys had a bet on us?" Jordan asked as we joined them at the high chairs around the beautiful kitchen island. Only two of their cousins and one of Jordan's friends were still there; everybody else had already gone.

"It's not my fault to have hoped my son wouldn't change girlfriends from one moment to another. I hope you called that poor girl," Mrs. Franklin said.

"The poor girl will be okay," Juliana said dramatically, and everybody laughed.

"Okay! Let's cut the cake before you two disappear," Mr. Franklin said, smiling at us.

I was sitting on the chair while Jordan stood between my legs, one hand resting on my thigh and the other on the island. I had one of my hands on his shoulder, trailing down to his chest, and the other playing with his hair.

"Are you leaving?" his mother asked, and Jordan nodded.

"Where are you going?"

"We'll be in Galveston for two days." With that, he cut the cake, and Juliana opened a bottle of champagne. We mingled for a little while before we left.

As we were leaving, Mrs. Franklin said, "Please try not to get pregnant. My heart cannot take any more surprises."

Everyone laughed, except me and her. I understood her message clearly. My past relationship earned me two amazing kids. It wouldn't be a surprise if I got pregnant again. Thank

God my mother made sure I took control of my birth plan the moment I gave birth to Liliana. I had been on birth control even though I hadn't been sexually active for two years.

Jordan opened the door of his car for me. Juliana promised to take my car back home the next day. We stopped at a few clothing stores and bought two pairs of shorts, a T-shirt, and a blouse. I also found two beautiful dresses, two pairs of shoes, hair ties, mascara, and a brow pencil. I picked up more makeup items and a backpack. Jordan also bought some things for himself and paid for everything.

After that, we went to a grocery store and grabbed a few drinks and some snacks. We had about an hour and a half to reach our destination. It was already 10 p.m.

We started driving toward Galveston. After we finished shopping and Jordan filled up the gas, he was so gentle, treating me like a delicate flower. He held my hand as he drove. I brought his hand to my lips and kissed it. He let go, then placed his hand on my left breast, massaging it. My nipples were so hard. He pinched the one on the left, and a moan escaped my mouth. My body was electrified by Jordan's touch.

He moved his hand down to my thighs and slid it under my skirt, right in between my legs. His fingers started massaging my clit on top of my panties. I bit my lower lip as I looked at him. His eyes were glued to the road. I wasn't sure how he was multitasking like this.

"Jordan," his name escaped my lips as I closed my eyes. His hand felt so good.

We reached a red light. Jordan slid two fingers inside my pussy as he stopped the car.

"Oooh! My God."

My breathing got heavier. His fingers felt so good inside me, and with his thumb massaging my clit, I placed my hands on the dashboard and parted my legs wide, giving him full access. The two-minute wait for a green light was enough to make me come hard.

By the time the car behind us started honking, my orgasm was all over Jordan's fingers. My legs were shaking and weak from the intensity. All I could do was gasp for air.

Jordan put his fingers inside his mouth, licking off my come as he drove.

"Give me your panties," Jordan said in a deep, sexy voice that turned me on all over again.

I took my panties off and handed them to him. He put them on his nose like a mask.

I laughed so hard. The fact that he had my panties on his face turned me on again, as if what he just did with his fingers wasn't already enough. I untied the knot behind my T-shirt and took off my bra, releasing my breasts. My nipples were hard and painful. I was so horny, like I had never been before.

Jordan always awakened my sexual desires.

He got off the road at the next right, and before I regained my full strength, he parked in a Cinemax theater parking lot. There were only a few cars, and the parking lot was dark. He parked on the darker side.

"Hold on," he said, getting out of the car. He put the panties inside his pocket. He turned around to the passenger door and opened it while looking around. I got out of the car holding his hand. He clashed his lips with mine, kissing me like his life depended on it, and I kissed him back, tasting my own cum on his mouth.

He opened the back door of the car. "Get in, sweetheart."

I got in as he ordered, sitting in the middle as he entered behind me and closed the door. We started kissing while he slid his hands under my t-shirt, onto my boobs, massaging them and pinching my nipples, sending electrical shots all over my body.

"Mmmmmh! J."

He moved his lips to my neck now, but still kept his hands on my breasts.

"I will be right back," he said.

I just nodded. I was already bothered; my mouth couldn't voice a word anymore.

He got in front and pulled the front seats forward, which created more room at the back.

"Lie down, sweetheart," he said.

I lay with my back on the car seat. He pulled my legs up, spreading them apart, and put his mouth between my legs, eating me up.

"Ooooooh! Yes, yes, yes, mmmmmmh!" I screamed as I reached climax again with his mouth on my sex. He used his tongue to fuck me, then he sucked my clit, teasing it with his teeth sometimes. I was on the verge of coming for the second time when he let go of my sex and moved to my breasts. He pulled the t-shirt off, exposing my chest. He sucked my nipples one after another. I didn't notice when he took his pants down. He slid his penis inside my pussy.

"Oooh! My God."

I squeezed the hair on his head, which was on my breast.

"You are so tight, so perfect, baby," he said to my ear as he pushed himself deeper. He moved back to a sitting position, still inside me, and then he pressed my legs together, pushing them to the side. He held my thighs together and put another hand on my waist and started moving in and out a little faster, thrusting strongly this time, driving both of us to climax and giving me a double orgasm.

I lay there with my hand up on my head, looking at Jordan's chest. He was shirtless. I had no idea at what point he took his hood off. He looked so good, and his penis was still semi-erect. He smiled at me, completely aware that I was checking him out. He opened the compartment between the front seats and got a bag of wipes, then started cleaning me up gently. God, he looked so sexy. He was so handsome; I didn't know how I survived the two years without him with me like this.

"FYI, I don't mind if I left little Jordan in you," he said, and we both laughed.

"You wish. Well, sorry darling, I'm on birth control," I answered as I pulled down my skirt and put on my t-shirt while

Jordan finished putting his hooded sweater back on as he got out. He got in my seat in front and pulled it back.

"Please put your bra back on before I forget we need to get to Galveston like yesterday," he said, throwing my bra at me playfully.

I smiled so hard it hurt from how happy I was at that moment. My breasts were the part of my body that I didn't like because of how big they were, but the fact that Jordan loved them made me feel so amazing and so proud to have these two right then.

We got back in our seats. I took the bag of snacks and took out a bag of chips, feeling hungry already. I opened it, ate some, and fed Jordan some. I fed the whole bag of chips to both of us. As Jordan drove, he put on some soft music, and in like thirty minutes, I fell asleep.

When I woke up, we were parked in front of the hotel in Galveston.

"I'm so sorry, I fell asleep," I said to him as he opened the door for me.

"It's okay. I love watching you sleeping," he said, smiling.

I put my hand around his neck and kissed him.

"I love you," I said as we let go.

"I love you too, sweetheart."

I loved it when he called me sweetheart; it brought butterflies to my stomach.

He carried all our things inside. I just carried the snack bags and my purse. We checked in at the front and headed to the room.

We were going to the fourth floor, so when we got in the elevator, Jordan didn't want to waste any time. He pinned me to the wall, started kissing me, and squeezed my ass with his free hand. I was already turned on from the kiss we shared in the car. My body responded to him like a magnet. Jordan made me feel so good. He kissed me the right way, touched me in the right places, and made me feel amazing.

We dropped everything at the door when we got into the room. We took each other's clothes off so quickly; in a few minutes, we were on the bed. This time, he was not so gentle; he thrust inside me faster and harder. I spread my legs open under him, taking him whole. We both came so hard, still not getting enough of each other. We went into it again and again; we had sex on the bed so many times I lost count. We went to take a shower after, both of us smelling like sex and sweat. We had sex there under the water too. It was so amazing. We fell asleep after that for a few hours.

I woke up the next morning from a dream that Jordan was eating my pussy, only to find him doing just that. His head was between my legs, eating my clit like breakfast.

"Oooh! Yeah! Jordan." I raised my hips, going crazy with how amazing his lips felt.

"Mmmmmh!" I let out a breath as he moved his body up, kissing my breasts while his dick slid inside my opening.

"Good morning, sweetheart," he said, kissing my ear. Then he slid his tongue inside my ear for a few seconds. My insides exploded, and I came so hard, but he didn't stop. He kept thrusting faster and harder until we came together.

"Are you trying to get me addicted or something?" I said breathlessly.

"Addicted to me?" he asked, smiling, and I nodded shyly.

"I hope you do, because I already am." We both smiled and kissed.

"Come on, sweetheart, I ordered breakfast for us."

We sat on the couch naked, not bothering to put on any clothes. I noticed he had put our things away from the door where we dropped them last night. We ate in silence at first, just looking at each other. I felt some soreness between my legs after having so much sex in one night, but I knew I wasn't going to stop for anything, not now that I had this beautiful man in front of me.

"So, you really want to have a baby with me?" I asked, remembering what he said in the car earlier.

"I do. Actually, I've fantasized about Liliana being mine. I wish we had made a baby that night." He smiled, looking at me while biting his bread, making eating bread seem so sexy.

"That night was the best night, even though I didn't like how it ended," I said as I drank the orange juice.

"Have you been with anyone after that night?" he asked seriously, looking at me like he was trying to read my mind.

"You killed all my fantasies that night and built a very high bar of expectations. My body has only been craving you," I said, getting on his lap. I could see him start to get hard again.

"So you mean no one has touched you like this?" he asked, touching my clit with his fingers.

"No! Jordan, why didn't you ever let me know how you felt about me in high school?" I asked the question that had been in my head since Pablo told me all those crazy, painful words.

Jordan took his hand off my clit and looked me in the eyes.

"When you came to our school, the whole group liked you," he said.

"Wait…you mean the whole group?" I asked, surprised.

"Well, maybe not the whole group, but a number of us. Robert, Nick, Jade… others never confirmed, but we always talked about how pretty you were. And Pablo went ahead and got the girl, so we stayed away. It was like a silent bro code never to go after each other's girls."

Wow. So now I understood.

"I had no idea." I held his cheeks between my palms. "What did you guys see? I was a nerd and such an uninteresting human being," I said.

"You are so beautiful, Leoncia, and these breasts and that ass are just a bonus." We both laughed.

"Now they are all yours," I said seductively, already bothered and wet. We had sex again on the couch, with me controlling the thrust, moving my hips up and down. Then he turned me around and fucked me so hard, I swear I forgot my name for a few minutes.

We went to the beach later. We ate corn while walking around. We enjoyed the beach so much, just relaxing with our hands entwined the whole time, kissing once in a while, here and there.

We got back to the room around four p.m., showered, and got ready to go out for dinner. We got dressed up. I wore a short blue dress that held my body so well. He wore black pants and a white shirt with short sleeves; he looked so handsome.

We went to a beautiful restaurant. This was our first date together. I took a lot of selfies, both by myself and with him. He also took a few pictures of me and saved one of just me as his wallpaper. My wallpaper had my kids, and for some reason, I didn't feel like taking them out.

After we came back, we made love under the sheets one more time before we both fell into a deep sleep, tired from all the sex we had had in twenty-four hours. I had never had that much sex before in one day, but I wasn't complaining.

The next day, we woke up and left because Jordan needed to go to LA for some business venture. He also needed to meet his team, sign some documents, and get the schedule for the next football season, as they would start training for the game soon.

***

Five months had passed since I became Jordan's girlfriend, and it had been amazing. Jordan was amazing, attentive, and super romantic. He permanently moved to LA now, but that hadn't stopped us. We talked every single day. We video chatted, sexted, and saw each other every other week. I usually went to LA, and sometimes he came to Houston. Our sex drive was enhanced every time we met.

I found a new job, but I always made sure I was off on the weekends, when I had to go to LA. On my birthday this year, he sent me a ticket to go to LA. We spent my birthday weekend together, visiting different places in LA. It was fun, and we ended the day with a passionate night of endless lovemaking.

We spent two nights and a day together. Before I left, we went to different places in LA, just enjoying ourselves. Jordan always made me happy; he was so good at everything he did.

Two weeks ago was his first game of the season. We had talked about it so many times, but I couldn't go because I was doing my finals that weekend. They won, and I was so proud, but I felt guilty for not being able to be there on the first important day of his career. I was able to go to some of his other games.

In December, I graduated. Jordan came to surprise me, but he left at midnight after we spent some time alone in a hotel because he had to be up early exercising in the morning.

His team made the playoffs. Jordan's birthday was in January. His family traveled to LA that weekend to celebrate. The plan was to go to the game, then have dinner with him. I got to LA a day before his parents. I stayed in his apartment, which he was renting, so we wouldn't spend all our time in hotels when I was there. I couldn't see him much because he and his team were exercising for the game the next day.

His big game fell on the day before his birthday, so I knew that night would be one of the big celebrations after midnight. I received a call from my mother in the morning on the day of his game, informing me that my baby girl was in the hospital and couldn't breathe. I took the next available flight and went back home. I talked to Jordan, and he understood, but it didn't ease my guilt about not being there for his birthday. Plus, his team won, so it was a double celebration. This guy had been treating me like a queen, making me the center of his world, and in return, I did nothing but disappoint him.

I got to the hospital where my baby girl was admitted. Her health wasn't okay. She showed the symptoms of asthma, and they had been giving her medication through an inhaler to reduce the symptoms.

A week later, I went to see the pulmonologist, and they confirmed that my daughter might have asthma. She was prescribed an inhaler to use at home. My mother told me this had started a few months ago, but I hadn't realized because, lately, I had been leaving the kids with my mother a lot. Sometimes, she felt bad telling me because she didn't want to spoil my relationship and the private time I had with Jordan.

I fought with my mother about it because I felt like I had been neglecting my kids for my selfish desire to be loved. I didn't tell Jordan how I felt, but I reduced the trips to LA because I wanted to be physically available to my kids. I was their mother, not my mother. I felt guilty for putting them second and placing my desire first. These kids had only me. I was no longer the eighteen-year-old who got pregnant and let my parents and Pablo's parents plan my life for me. I was a twenty-two-year-old single mother with two amazing kids who had only me to look after them.

I loved Jordan a lot, but my kids would always come first.

Today was the Super Bowl. Jordan wanted me to go (his team got to the Super Bowl, and I was so proud of him), but I couldn't make it. Liliana had been sick. Last week, I took her to the emergency room, and we spent six hours there after she had another asthma attack.

His parents couldn't go either. His father had a car accident last month and had been in a wheelchair since. Unfortunately, he was paralyzed. His legs didn't work now. Only Juliana and some of their family and friends went.

Mrs. Franklin called me and invited me to her house. She said she was going to host the Super Bowl, and I should go. My daughter felt better, and because I wasn't going out of town, I decided to go watch the Super Bowl with the Franklin family. I talked to Jordan in the morning; he was so excited for the game. I wished they would win.

The house wasn't crowded; it was just Jordan's parents, his aunt, and two cousins. We watched the game while eating and drinking. Mrs. Franklin always hosted the best parties. When the game ended, Jordan's team lost, but it felt like a win since they hadn't even made it to the playoffs in the past three years. The fact that he got them to the Super Bowl and secured second place was an achievement for them. He also won Quarterback of the Year and Best New Player of the Year, and I was so proud of him. This was his greatest accomplishment, considering it was his first season.

"Well, I dedicate all this to my family and my girlfriend Leoncia. I love you all so much," he said when the press congratulated him.

Juliana screamed next to him, so proud. I knew I should have been there, and the guilt of not giving Jordan what he wanted and needed from a girlfriend who should be present was killing me every day. I knew he deserved better, but I loved him, and I was selfish, especially when it came to him.

My phone rang, and it was Jordan calling. He was still on the stage, and I guessed he couldn't wait to talk to me. Again, it should have been me calling him before he did. I picked up.

"Hallow! Babe, I am so proud," I said, shaking off the guilt.

"Thank you so much. How is Liliana?" he asked.

I knew he cared more about her than her father. Pablo hadn't come to visit his daughter even once since she got sick. Only his mother came. She said he was in Asia now. I wasn't sure what country, and I didn't care.

"She is better now. The inhaler they gave us this time is working," I answered. "Tell me how you feel?" I asked.

"I am okay, and I miss you terribly," he said.

I missed him too, so much. It had been two months since we were together. It was in December when I last saw him. We talked every day, but my body ached for him.

"I miss you too, darling. When are you coming back?"

"I will be there on Friday, sweetheart," he answered.

"Wow! I will be waiting for you."

We talked a little bit about random stuff, such as how his day went and about some of his teammates who pissed him off somehow during the game. We ended the call, and I started getting ready to go when Mrs. Franklin called me.

"I was wondering if you have a spare moment. I would like to talk to you," she said.

"Yes, no problem." I followed her to the office. We sat on the couch facing each other.

"I want to talk to you about my son," she said, and I nodded. It wasn't a secret that she never liked me, but we had tolerated each other for Jordan's sake.

"It's obvious that we are the most important women in Jordan's life, and we both love him."

I nodded again, still wondering what she wanted.

"Also, I know you know that Jordan doesn't deserve a girlfriend like you," she said, standing up. "My son gives you everything. To him, you are the center of his existence. I have never seen him love anything like this, and I am afraid you will destroy him." She sat on one of the chairs across from me.

"You don't care about his feelings, or you don't show it enough. And I can't blame you. You're a mother, and your kids will always come first. But Jordan is my child, and it hurts me to see you giving him just leftovers." Tears ran down my cheeks as she continued talking.

"He is at the prime of his career. He needs a woman who is there a hundred percent or more. Someone who will make him feel loved and cared for. He works so hard for this relationship with you. My son has given you more than a normal man can give, but what did you give him? Disappointment and empty promises that you cannot keep."

"I want you to keep yourself in his position and tell me, would you date yourself? Is it fair to keep him hooked on you, knowing that he doesn't deserve this crap of a relationship you can offer?"

At this point, I was crying uncontrollably. I put my hands over my mouth so I wouldn't make noise. Mrs. Franklin made a lot of sense. It was true. I had been selfish and unfair.

"I don't know what you will decide to do. After all this, I know it is not up to me. But if you love my son even a little, please stop using him. Let him be free, free to find someone who will love him unconditionally. The way he truly deserves. As a mother, that is all I ask of you. Spare my son from the disappointments. We both know there will be more to come, and he will never be your first priority. To you, Jordan will always come last while you are his everything."

With that, Mrs. Franklin stood up and left me there.

I calmed myself down a little and then left. I didn't say goodbye to anyone. I just left, went home, and cried some more.

Friday came. Jordan went to his parents' house first. He picked me up around six p.m.; he had already booked a hotel downtown. We missed each other so much, so we didn't waste time when we got to the hotel. That night, I tried to memorize every touch, every kiss, how it felt making love to Jordan because I was still not sure what I would do.

I knew I had to do something. I couldn't be selfish forever. It wasn't fair to anyone. I was there in a hotel room with the most amazing man on earth, getting fucked senselessly. But I still worried about my daughter. It wasn't fair for them both. My daughter needed a mother who was always there for her, while this man also needed a woman who was emotionally and unconditionally in love with him. I couldn't help but feel guilt. I wished I could divide myself, leaving one half with Liliana and the other half with Jordan. But that was impossible, and I was going crazy. They both meant so much to me.

I couldn't sleep well. I woke up before Jordan. I looked at him sleeping peacefully. He was so handsome, and he made me so happy, but did I make him happy? I asked myself. I loved him, but I also loved my kids, and I was all they had. Jordan could find another woman, another me, but my kids would never have another mother. I was chosen to be their mother so I could love them unconditionally and protect them, even from my own desires.

"Are you watching me while I sleep?" Jordan brought me back from my thoughts.

"It's your fault for being so handsome," I said, kissing him.

"What time is it?"

"Past eight a.m."

He stood up and went to the bathroom. He was naked. I looked at him, admiring what I saw. Jordan's body was so perfect, like a piece of art. I heard him take a shower, and I started cleaning up the room. We always messed up the room after our lovemaking and sex sessions. We did it in every corner of the room, and I still didn't know if I could let go of how good Jordan made me feel.

I went down to the lobby and grabbed breakfast for us. Jordan was out of the shower, wearing only his boxers.

"Hi! I was about to call you," he said, smiling.

"Sorry, I didn't tell you I was getting breakfast."

We started eating our breakfast, and then Jordan took out his laptop.

"Sweetheart, I want to show you something." He finished his coffee quickly and then started scrolling through his emails. He clicked on one of the attachments in an email he opened, and it contained pictures of houses.

I looked at him, not understanding what he was showing me.

"I've been looking for houses I want us to buy. Take a look and tell me which one you like. My father's real estate agent sent them to me." He kissed me on the mouth, smiling, but I didn't smile back. I was shocked.

"A house? Wait, what do you mean?" I asked, standing up.

"I mean, buy a house, move in together. Me, you, the kids. It's going to be amazing," he said, smiling and holding my waist.

"No!" The word escaped my mouth, and Jordan frowned, looking at me.

"No? You don't want to live with me?" he asked.

"Jordan, this is not working. We need to break up. It hasn't been working for a while," I said, slicing my own heart with the words I just spoke. I sat down on the bed, holding my head in my hands. Jordan stood there, looking at me like I had just spoken a foreign language.

"Break up? Is this because of the house? Then forget I said anything. We cannot break up, Cia." He pulled me up from the bed, hugging me and kissing me. "Please, we can't break up, my love," he said. Tears rolled down my cheeks.

"Jordan, I'm done being selfish. I love you so much. I can't ruin your life. We both know I'm not right for you," I said.

"No, I don't know that. Leoncia, you're my everything," he said.

"And that's the problem, Jordan. My life is so complicated right now. I have a lot going on to be the right woman for you. And I can't just take everything from you. I can't promise you even my full attention."

"Sweetheart, I don't expect anything from you. You don't have to give me anything. To be with you is a privilege, and that's all I need," he said, hugging me tight.

"I'm not worth it, Jordan. I'm never going to be the woman you deserve. It's better we end this now before we get bitter and hate each other," I said, getting myself out of his hold. But he pulled me to him and held me. I didn't want what happened with Pablo to repeat again, especially with Jordan. I wouldn't stand for him to hate me one day. It was better now, while he loved me, so it would be hard for him to hate me.

"Sweetheart, please, you can't do this. You can't be certain of what the future holds for us. We can be happy together." He looked me in the eyes, pleading.

"I can't promise to make you happy, Jordan. Tell me, Jordan, all those times I promised I would be there for you and couldn't make it. Weren't you disappointed? If you can tell me you didn't feel bad that I wasn't there, then please don't lie to me," I said, looking him in the eyes.

"Yes, I was disappointed. But I understand, and it's not a problem for me," he said, still looking at me, begging me with his eyes not to do this.

"For now, it's not a problem. Jordan, this is how it's going to be. Me not showing up when you need me and not being able to give you what you need, unconditional love. Because my children will always come first, whether we like it or not, you will always be my last priority. And that's not fair. I love you so much. Trust me, it's better we end this now, when we don't hate each other, than later," I said.

We stayed quiet, looking at each other for a minute.

Jordan kissed me, and I kissed him back. He wasn't gentle. We were both crying, but we didn't break the kiss. We moved to the bed. He took off my top and slid down the shorts, along with the pants I was wearing. He looked at me for a minute, as if memorizing my naked body, taking a screenshot in his brain.

"Oh my God. Aaaaaaaah!" I screamed as he thrust inside my opening, fucking me senselessly. He was rough and mad, but he felt so good, and I knew I couldn't let this desire cloud my judgment. Breaking things up with him was the best thing to do now.

He kept going even after we climaxed. He didn't stop, and we turned our bodies on with the friction between my pussy and his penis. It was like our bodies understood this might not happen again for a while or maybe never.

He let me go after he exploded the second time inside me and moved to the other side of the bed, crying. I had never seen him cry before.

"Jordan, I am so sorry," I said.

"Just leave, Leoncia. If that's what you want, I cannot stop you," he said, not looking at me.

"Can we still be friends, at least?" I asked, hoping I could keep that part of our relationship.

"I can't be your friend knowing I want more. If this is over, it needs to be over, Leoncia. I can't keep being in your life after this," he said, still not looking at me.

I got off the bed, put on my clothes, and then left with my heart broken into pieces.

Chapter VII:
The Taste of True Love

It had been three years since that morning. Jordan had blocked my number and me on all his social media accounts where he used to follow me. Juliana kept talking to me, but our friendship died when she moved to New York to pursue her modeling career.

Their father died six months after we broke up. I went to his burial ceremony, but I couldn't talk to Jordan. There were so many people. I just left a card for him with my name on it, hoping he would know how sorry I was for his loss and everything that had happened between us.

His team kept doing well. His team won the Super Bowl three times in a row. I was so proud of him. He hadn't dated anyone publicly. There had been some speculation and rumors about him dating a few women, but nothing was confirmed until last fall, when it was revealed that he was dating an actress. She was so beautiful and the luckiest woman to be with the most amazing man I had ever known in my life.

His mother moved to LA with him, and they sold their house in Houston after Juliana moved to New York five months later, erasing any trace of him.

I graduated and landed a really good-paying job. I was able to clean up my credit and rent a three-bedroom apartment. I moved in with my kids. My mother wasn't happy at first, but she agreed that I needed to start taking responsibility as a mother and care for my children. She always came to visit. I think she spent more time at my apartment than hers. Her business was doing well. She expanded her beauty supply business; now she had two more shops, and she was thriving.

Pablo came back to the USA two years ago and was stationed in Hawaii. He got married last year, and they were expecting a baby. He had returned to his kids' lives, but he and I didn't communicate at all. His mother was still the middle person who transferred messages between us. He came to Houston this February and stayed for the whole week. I let the kids go with him, and he was the one who brought them back. That was the last time I saw him. He had changed. He had gained a lot of weight and was no longer as skinny as he used to be. He had grown a beard and had long hair. He looked completely different. I kind of wondered what I ever saw in him. He was not the kind of man I would be attracted to anymore, not after I had tasted what it was like to be with Jordan.

I still owned the car Jordan had bought for me. My mother kept telling me to sell it so I could move on. She felt like I kept it in the hope that he would come back. I didn't tell my mother the details of why we broke up, and she didn't ask. So I understood when she thought I was hoping he would come back. I knew he wouldn't. He might take me back if I wanted him to, but he had cut all ties, sending a message that he wanted nothing to do with me.

Jordan's life was the complete opposite of mine. He was famous, rich, and had access to all these beautiful, gorgeous women in LA and across the USA: actresses, models, influencers, and so many more. Women loved him. Even teenagers were crazy about him, and I couldn't blame them. Jordan was handsome, so good-looking, and he only got better with age. And the fact that I knew he was good in bed... no woman could be with him and not fall for him.

My daughter was better now. We had been in the emergency room several times, and she had been hospitalized a couple of times, but the episodes had reduced. Both my kids were in school, my boy had started first grade, and my girl was in kindergarten. My life had become a routine. We woke up in the morning, got ready, went to school, and to work. My mother picked them up. Sometimes Pablo's mother picked them up, and sometimes, after work, I would go and pick them up. We went home, did homework, ate dinner, showered, and went to sleep. I was fine with my life. I was always happy when I saw my kids happy. On weekends, we would go to the park or spend time with my mother at her house.

My mother now had a boyfriend, a very nice man. He loved her so much, and I was happy for her. My aunt got married two years ago and moved to Alabama with her husband.

My love life was next to non-existent. I had tried dating several times, but all of them were unsuccessful. I remember that a year after Jordan and I broke up, I met a guy. He was my coworker, Michael, and he used to adore and care deeply for me. He would sometimes bring me snacks, breakfast, or lunch, and I liked it. We exchanged numbers, and I really thought he was cool and nice. I knew, in a way, I had been looking for someone who kind of reminded me of Jordan, and Michael's behavior toward me did.

A month after we met, I had an accident. My car was taken to be fixed for ten days. Michael picked me up every morning and dropped me off after work all those days. So when he asked me to go out with him, I agreed, and I was excited. He picked me up and drove us to his house. That was a surprise for me because I thought we were going out, maybe to a restaurant. He said he cooked dinner, and we ate. Surprisingly, the dinner was really good and tasty. I felt lucky for a moment, thinking I might have found a man who could cook. My cooking wasn't good, and I was fine with it, as long as my kids liked my food, I was okay.

After we finished dinner, he started kissing me, and at that point, I hadn't had sex for more than a year. I was horny, and I liked the guy, so I let him kiss me, and I had sex with him. The sex was good. But for someone who had experienced the level of mind-blowing intimacy that I had, it was nothing. I knew I might never experience love like that again and might have to settle for something less, and I was okay with it.

After we left his apartment, Michael started planning for us to meet again the next day, saying he would cook me his favorite food. So I decided to ask him if this meant we were dating, if his inviting me to his place again meant we were together.

He was so surprised, saying, "I didn't know you were like those girls who think if a man sleeps with them, then they have to date."

Then he said, "We don't need to label anything that doesn't need a label."

He explained further that he had a lot going on in his life and couldn't be in a relationship at the moment. He said it was better if we just kept doing what we did, without any strings attached, and that was it. I never talked to him again until I got my current job three months later.

Since then, I have had flings, trying to connect with other people romantically, but they have been unsuccessful. I joined several dating apps, but the conversations went nowhere. I had gone on dates, but no one felt right. My body felt as though it had been frozen for a while. I hadn't felt excited by anyone. Scott was supposed to be salvation and my hope to love again, but now all that was messed up.

I was so tired of trying this dating thing. For a while, I thought I was okay. But my body was thirsty, and my heart was starving for love.

Present day.

I got home almost at midnight. I had no strength left in me. I had to work tomorrow, and life needed to go on. I opened my chats with Scott, reading all the texts over and over again. I wished I could call him, but I wasn't sure he would pick up. I couldn't believe I had lost the most incredible man in the world just because I didn't tell him about my kids. Why didn't I tell him about them? I had no idea.

Scott was exactly the man I wanted and needed in my life. He had just declared his love for me before I ruined everything.

I cried myself to sleep for the rest of the week. If only I had known that he would turn out to be the one, the one who would make me love again, feel the way he made me feel. I would have done everything differently. I replayed our time together every second. I didn't know how to move forward.

On Friday, I asked my mother to pick up the kids, and as always, she came to my rescue. I did not share what had happened with my mother. I was ashamed of the fact that I had messed up the chance to be happy.

I ordered food and bought a bottle of wine on my way back home. I ate and drank the whole bottle, causing me to fall asleep on the couch.

I woke up tired and with a headache. I decided to go to the store to buy food and some more drinks. I had a long day alone today. I took a quick shower and then wore sweatpants, a T-shirt, and a sweater.

I arrived at the store and selected some items, adding them to my cart. Then I heard a voice from my phone. I opened it to check, and it was a text, but it was actually a notification from the Ring camera app. I had bought the camera when I moved into that house. As a single mother, I felt I needed that for protection.

I couldn't believe what I saw when I opened the app. It was Scott standing in front of my door, ringing the doorbell. I searched his name, calling him, not believing what I saw.

"Hello!" he answered with his deep voice.

"Is that you? Is that really you at my door?"

"Yes, baby girl. Can you open the door? We need to talk."

"I… I am not home; I will be there in a few minutes. Please don't leave," I said, walking so fast to my car, leaving everything in the cart where I had been standing.

"Okay! Drive safe, I will be waiting."

"Okay!" I hung up as I started the car. I drove as fast as possible. It was Saturday, almost noon, and it looked like everyone was out today.

I got home in about ten minutes. I ran out of the car after I parked in the garage, closing the garage door with the remote as I got inside. I left everything on the table, then ran to the restroom I had downstairs, looking at myself in the mirror. I didn't look so bad. Thank God I had showered before going to the store.

I ran to the door and opened it, and there he was in front of me. I wasn't sure why he was here, but all I could think about was kissing him. I missed him terribly. I jumped on him, wrapping my hands around his shoulders and my thighs around his waist. He held my waist tightly with his strong arms. I closed the gap between our faces and kissed him, not sure he would kiss me back, but he did, while moving inside. He stopped walking when we hit the wall.

I got down from him but still held his head, and he had to bend down as we kissed again.

"You are here."

"I am, darling. Please forgive me for the horrible things I said," he said.

"No, forgive me for not telling you sooner about my kids."

"It's okay. You are entitled to your privacy, and you chose to share with me when you were ready. I'm just sorry for the way I reacted," he said, and I couldn't believe he was saying that.

"You understand me?" I asked, not sure of what was happening at that moment.

"I understand you, baby girl," he said, kissing me, then added, "Now would you still want to be my girlfriend?"

I smiled first, then kissed him again and again.

"So?" he asked, and I laughed.

"Didn't the kisses answer your question? Yes, Scott, I would love to be your girlfriend."

He kissed me so passionately, I didn't remember how long we stayed kissing. I couldn't explain how I felt. It was like I was dreaming. Was this really happening? If it was a dream, I hoped I wouldn't wake up.

I held his hand as we broke from the kiss. By this time, he had dropped his bag where we were standing. I led us upstairs to my room. I knew it wasn't so clean, but all I wanted now was him. I would worry about other stuff later. I missed him so much.

"I miss you terribly," I said as I took off his jacket and shirt. Then I traced his chest with my fingers, admiring how strong and beautiful he looked and felt.

"I miss you a lot, Leo. I love you so much," he said, kissing me and taking off my clothes.

We took each other's clothes off in a few seconds. Scott moved backward after I lost my last piece of clothing, leaving me completely naked in front of him.

"I can't believe you are mine," he said, and I smiled.

"Let me show you that I am."

I reached for his hands and pushed him onto the bed, then climbed on top of him. I kissed him on the mouth for a few seconds, then started kissing my way down, spending extra time on his neck, sucking his skin so hard I might have left my mark there. I loved leaving love bites on men; it looked good and empowering, reminding them of you for a couple of days.

I moved down to his hard chest, kissing it all over and sucking his little breasts. I could hear him moan, but I wasn't done with him yet. I moved down, cupping his long and hard-as-rock penis in my hands, stroking him slowly. I looked at him, locking eyes with him, as I slid his length inside my mouth.

I had done this before, but I was on a mission to make this moment feel amazing for this amazing man on my bed. I closed my eyes as I sucked his penis, moving my mouth up and down in the same rhythm as my hands, using my tongue and lips to eat him up like a lollipop. I occasionally let his length all the way down my throat, knowing he would enjoy that.

As I knew he was getting close to exploding, I increased the friction and sucked him even harder.

"Leoncia," he held my hair as he screamed my name, then exploded, spraying his cum all over my face.

I smiled, satisfied with my little mission, as I walked to the bathroom to wash my face.

As I was finishing up drying my face with a towel, Scott got in and, without a word, pulled up my right leg to the top of the sink, making me bend down, holding on to the sink for support. Then I felt him push his penis into my open pussy, which was already wet for him.

"Oooh! Yes, yes, mmmmh," I screamed as he started thrusting in and out, faster and increasing the pace each time. I came within minutes, but Scott was not done with me. He picked me up, carried me back to the bedroom, and laid me down on the bed. Then he buried his mouth between my legs, eating me out, swallowing all the juices that came from the orgasm he had just given me in the bathroom.

He kept going, using his lips, tongue, and fingers all together, creating magic. In a few minutes, I was shaking again, screaming his name as I orgasmed so hard. But nope, he didn't stop. I held his head; if he had hair on it, I would have pulled it at this point. He made me feel so good and high, if you asked me my name, I might not have been able to tell you.

I slid my legs on his back and squeezed them tightly to fight the pressure that felt so good. With that, he released my pussy, spreading me wide. I was already so close. He pulled one of my legs to his shoulder and pushed himself inside me. I screamed as loud as I could, feeling another orgasm, but he kept going through it, thrusting faster and harder until we both reached climax together. Tears escaped my eyes with the pressure. I had never experienced this level of intimacy; it was amazing and out of this world. Scott felt so good. He was so perfect.

"You are crying, my love. Did I hurt you?" he asked, worried.

"No! I am so happy. I can't believe I am yours. Scott, I love you so much."

"You have been mine since the day I liked your profile. And I love you more," he said.

"Well, that's still debatable. I think I love you more."

"Well, I am the one who traveled from New Hampshire, so I think I'm winning this." We both laughed.

"By the way, how did you know where I live?"

"Someone sent me your driver's license a couple of weeks ago." Of course, it had my address. That's smart.

"So, you've really turned out to be not only a scammer who stole my heart but also a stalker whom I really love," I said, remembering the day I told him my fears after I shared my driver's license with him.

We kissed again and again before we went back to it, making passionate love. Our bodies connected perfectly, understanding each other's needs and getting the satisfaction we needed while craving more each time.

After a few rounds, we took a shower together. I ordered food after that, and then we sat downstairs in the dining room to eat. I was wearing his shirt. I loved wearing my man's shirt because it made me feel closer to him, smelling his scent on me. He was wearing only his boxers, and I didn't have any pants on. He fed me, and I fed him. We kissed every few minutes. It was so much fun. I was so lucky. I still couldn't believe I had woken up this morning heartbroken. Now my heart was filled with joy and happiness.

"Mmmmmh," I breathed in, trying not to hold my breath as he picked an ice cube from the soda cup, put it in his mouth, then put my left breast inside his mouth, sucking it with the ice between his lips.

"Scott!" I called him breathlessly as he moved to the other breast and did the same thing. I couldn't take it anymore. At this point, I jumped on his lap, cupping his face with my hands, quite aware that my ass cheeks were exposed because his shirt had ridden up as I stretched my legs around him. As the horny boyfriend he was, he cupped them with his hands as we kissed.

We were so lost in the kiss that we didn't hear someone opening the door. My baby girl's voice stopped me as she called, "Mama!"

I jumped off Scott as fast as I could, buttoning the few buttons that were open, and she came running to me. I hugged her, and her brother followed behind. Then my mother appeared.

"Who are you?" Liliana asked Scott, surprised. I could see Scott holding his hands on his lap, probably hiding his boner. I picked up a pillow and gave it to him before kneeling down to Liliana's level.

"This is Scott, Mama's friend," I told her. Liliana was always curious and had a lot of questions, unlike Antonio, who was quiet and rarely asked questions.

"Where are your clothes?" she asked again, surprised, and Scott laughed, causing me to laugh too.

"Mama, I thought you were bringing them back tomorrow?" I asked, avoiding her eyes.

My mother grabbed the blanket from the case we put it on, then walked over to Scott and gave it to him. "I didn't know you had company. We're here to grab Antonio's favorite toy," she said, looking at me with questioning eyes.

"Mama, this is my boyfriend Scott. Scott, meet my mother," I introduced them. At this time, the kids were already running around.

"Nice to meet you, ma'am," Scott said to my mother, raising his hand to her.

"Sorry, I am not shaking that hand today. I have no idea where it has been," she said, and we both laughed. "But it was nice to meet you, too."

She turned around and grabbed Antonio's favorite toy.

"Let's go, kids, say bye to Mama and her friend," she said, walking towards the door. I was glad her boyfriend didn't come in with her, but he would know all about it. Between my mother and Liliana, no secret could be kept.

"Bye, Mama," the kids said, hugging me. Then they followed my mother out.

"They are so adorable. Are they twins?" Scott asked, and I realized I hadn't told him about my kids.

"No! They are one year apart. Antonio is my first, and then Liliana," I answered.

"Wow! Just like my sister Savannah and me. We are one year apart. People used to think we were twins," he said.

So Scott was the firstborn in his family of five kids, and he was the only boy, followed by Savannah (35), Sylvia (31), Vanessa (28), and Annabelle (22).

"For sure, it feels like they were twins," I said, sitting on his lap.

"What about their father? Is he in the picture?" he asked seriously.

"Not directly, but he is somehow. The kids know him, and that's enough."

"He lives here in Houston?" he asked, looking at me. I saw a hint of jealousy spreading across his face.

"He lives in Hawaii. He has this whole new life with his new wife."

"Perfect," he said, smiling.

"Listen, I feel nothing for that man. Our experience together ended horribly, and our two angels are the two best reasons we can even bear to be in each other's sight. So you have nothing to worry about," I said, kissing his cheek and smiling.

"What happened?" he asked. I debated whether I should tell him for a second, then a realization hit me that this was the man I loved, and he loved me. I should be able to tell him everything.

"He cheated on me so many times, and when he found out I was pregnant for the second time, he was so mad and left. So I decided to sleep with his ex-best friend, and he couldn't stand that I cheated. But at that point, even I was in the realization that our marriage was already dead."

"You guys were married?" That was one more thing I hadn't told him. I hoped he wasn't tired of my secrets by now.

"Before you get mad, that marriage doesn't mean anything anymore. That's why I sometimes forget it. We were eighteen and pregnant. Under the influence of our parents, we got married. But Pablo and I were not ready to get married."

"Are you still married?" he asked. I could see concern in his eyes.

"We divorced years ago. He is married now," I said, making sure it was clear to him there was nothing between me and my babies' dad.

"This friend you cheated with, is he still in the picture?" he asked seriously.

"No. He and I ended a few years ago."

I ended it there because I didn't like talking about Jordan. He was still a sensitive subject to me. I didn't think I still loved him, but I knew I cared a lot about him; he was the most important person in my love life. Plus, his sister still spoke to me occasionally, and I still had the car he had bought me. I really needed to trade that car and buy another.

"So you dated him?"

"Yes, but it never worked out," I said, smiling.

"I'm glad it didn't. By the way, remind me not to cheat on you," he said playfully.

"Don't even joke about that, Scott. You cheat, and it's over," I said seriously.

"Honey! Your ex was stupid to cheat on an incredible woman like you."

He put me on his lap and held my hands. Now we were sitting on the couch.

"Leo, you are everything I have been looking for in a woman and more. I will never look at any other woman again but you. No one exists but you only."

He kissed me, and I kissed him back.

"So, dating a woman with two kids was what you were looking for?" I asked, smiling.

"No, that's more like a bonus."

We both laughed. I felt so happy and complete. My life was so different today, and now that I had finally found someone I really loved, I knew it wasn't going to be easy, but I would make sure we made it work.

"So what are we going to do with the miles between Houston and New Hampshire?" I asked, trying to move the conversation to the important things in our relationship, away from my past.

"I have a plan," Scott said.

I woke up in Scott's arms, my head resting on his chest on the side. One of my hands was under my head on his chest and the other around him, while one of his hands held me from the back all the way to my waist, with his fingers brushing the upper side of my ass.

We were both naked under the sheets, our legs entwined. It had been so long since I last woke up next to a man, a very handsome man.

Yesterday, we had spent a lot of time talking and came up with a plan that would ensure our relationship lasted. We agreed to be honest with each other if we didn't like something; also, communication had to be one of the main things to focus on

I gave Scott my mother's number, and he gave me his sister Savannah's number as our default contacts if we couldn't reach each other. Second, we explained our daily schedules to each other. We had only one hour difference, so time was not a big deal. I now knew that he always woke up early, around 5 a.m., worked out, and then got ready to go to the office. He always had meetings; as one of the directors, he had numerous meetings throughout the day.

Scott promised to come every other weekend, but we agreed that if we couldn't meet for three weeks or a month, it was okay; we would always be in touch, both through voice and video calls.

We had many plans, including traveling together. In January, he had a work-related trip to New York, and he had already invited me to go with him for a week. Then in March, we were going to Dubai. I had never been out of the USA before; I was really looking forward to that trip already. He also said he would spend Christmas with his family, which was next week, but would come back for the New Year. I hoped his family, especially his mother, wouldn't hate me for that. I had had bad experiences with mothers-in-law, hating or not liking me.

I looked at him sleeping; he was so cute. He woke up, finding me looking at him.

"Are you checking me out?" he asked, smiling.

"Well, I can't blame my eyes. They like what they see," I said, smiling.

He pulled me to him and started kissing each side of my neck. We had made love and had sex a lot since he came yesterday; I had lost count. So far, I had had more sex in the last twenty-four hours than I had in the past couple of years since I broke up with Jordan.

My phone rang. It didn't stop Scott on his mission to make me come again. He was on my breasts again, sucking them one after the other.

"Stop," I said as I looked at the caller ID.

"Why?" he asked, continuing with what he was doing. I rolled my eyes back, feeling the sensation in my toes.

"It's my mother." I knew if I picked up with Scott's mouth where it was, she would figure out I was having sex.

"Good morning mom." I tried to make my voice firm and clear as my body adjusted to the emptiness of Scott's touch when he walked to the bathroom.

"Hi, baby. So, is your boyfriend still there?" she asked.

"Yes, what do you think, he woke up and left?" I asked, smiling.

"I never see you with a boyfriend at your house. I don't know how it works," she said truthfully.

"That's fair. Yes, he is still here," I said.

"Okay! Put him on the phone."

"Why?"

"Just put him on the phone, baby."

Scott came back in from the bathroom before I got off the bed. I put the phone on speaker.

"He can hear you, Mama."

"Scott, when are you leaving?"

"Mom, what kind of questions are you asking my boyfriend?" I asked, surprised, and Scott smiled like it didn't bother him at all.

"I didn't mean it in a bad way. I just want to know. Jonathan is barbecuing tonight. I wanted to invite you two for dinner, but I have to make sure he will be able to come," my mother explained.

"I am still here. Thank you, we will come if it's okay with Leo," Scott answered my mother while smiling at me.

"Okay! We will be expecting you guys at seven p.m., with clothes on this time," she said, and we both laughed.

"Mama, please!" I said playfully.

"Thank you, Ma'am," Scott said.

"Please don't 'Ma'am' me. Just call me Doris. It's enough."

"Thank you, Mama." I ended the call, and Scott was smiling.

"What?"

"Your mother is so nice. I like her," he said.

"Well, I'm sure she likes you back."

Scott's phone rang as he was getting into bed next to me.

"Hallo!" He picked up, putting it on speaker so I could hear, and I heard a woman's voice.

"Are you on your way back already? Your mother is already asking for you," the woman said from the other side. Immediately, I knew it must be one of his sisters.

"Savannah, tell her I'm not coming today. Why do you keep her hopes up?"

"Because she needs to appreciate her other kids who are here," she said.

"What are you talking about, Savannah? Give Mom the phone," Scott asked seriously.

"Okay!" The phone stayed silent for a few seconds. "Mom, your son is on the phone. As I said, he is not coming for brunch today," we could hear Savannah saying. I wasn't sure I was supposed to listen to this conversation, but I stayed quiet.

"Hallo! Scott, are you coming?" his mother asked.

"I'm not coming, Mom. I told Savannah to tell you."

"Are you okay? You know Savannah exaggerates everything sometimes."

"I'm okay, Mom."

"Where are you?"

"Houston," he answered, smiling at me. I scooted onto his chest, and he kissed my forehead.

"As in Houston, Texas?"

"Yes, Mom."

"What are you doing there? Is it work? Your father keeps sending you all over," she asked and said, sounding surprised and sad.

"I am visiting my girlfriend."

"Wait, he said girlfriend!" We heard voices chatting on the other side.

"She said yes to forgive you?" Savannah asked on the other end. I started smiling. She really was something.

"Savannah, let me talk to my son, will you?" Mrs. Anderson said. "Is this the girl. The one from Facebook?"

Wow! He talked to his mother about me, I thought.

"Yes."

"Wow! Is she there? Can I say hi to her?" his mother said, and I suddenly got nervous.

"Hi, Mrs. Anderson," I said shyly, as if she could see me and know I was naked.

"Hallo, beautiful. You can call me Hilda."

"Okay," I said.

"Is my son treating you right? I know I raised him right."

"You sure did. He is amazing," I said.

"Thank you. Let me not take more of your time. It was nice to hear your voice. I hope I will see you soon," she said.

"I hope so."

"Okay! Scott, see you soon. Come home when you come back."

"Okay, Mom, I will." With that, he hung up.

"I am starving. Let me make breakfast." I put his shirt from last night on again. "You are leaving this shirt here; I already have history with it."

We both laughed, and he also put on his pants. We moved downstairs. He helped prepare breakfast while we kissed in between. It was so much fun, especially when you were this happy, the way I was.

We got to my mother's thirty minutes before 7 p.m. My mother and Jonathan were so nice to Scott. He got to meet my kids one more time. He played with them as I helped my mother set the table. I didn't know how I got this lucky, but Scott was the best thing that had happened to me. I was so happy.

Chapter VIII:
The Big Question

On Wednesday, Scott left, and it was so hard to say goodbye to each other. We kissed a lot, and that morning, we made love with such passion. It was incredible. I loved him so much. I didn't care how far we were, but I would make sure we stayed together for the rest of my life. Unless he let me go, I wasn't letting him go even if my life depended on it.

One month had passed. The holidays passed. Scott and I were still together and strongly in love. We both celebrated Christmas with our families, and he came for New Year's and spent it with my family. It was so much fun. We did fireworks, games, and my grandmother and aunt got to meet him.

I had just landed in New Hampshire. I was meeting his family tomorrow. I was so nervous about his family meeting me; I hoped they would like me. Also, I was so happy to be here—I missed Scott terribly. It had been three weeks without his physical touch. We talked every day, but it wasn't the same.

"Hi, babe," I said, running to him after I spotted him.

"Honey! I miss you," Scott said, kissing me, and I kissed him back.

"Welcome, darling. Let us go home." We got in the car, and he drove us to his home.

We arrived at this building; it was called *Anderson Estate*. The building was beautiful. He put the code in, and we drove to the parking space, which was marked 'Reserved,' and there was the Anderson name on it.

"Do you own this building?" I asked as he opened my door.

"Yes! It's one of my family properties," he said casually.

I didn't know what to say. I knew his family was extremely wealthy from what he had talked about. I had gathered that they owned a real estate company and had a couple of properties in New Hampshire, as well as some in New York. But wow.

"This building is so beautiful," I said as we entered the elevator.

"Thank you," he said while kissing my neck and hugging my waist.

"Mmmmm!" I took in the feeling of his lips on my neck. I had missed him so much.

We looked at each other as the elevator opened right inside his living room. We put the bags down and headed straight to the bedroom. We both had missed each other so much. I had actually never missed a man this way, but Scott wasn't like any other man I knew. I was actually addicted to him—his touch, his kisses. He fit inside me perfectly and made me feel so amazing every single time. I was so happy right then, like I had never been before, not even with Jordan. Trust me, I loved Jordan, and he was amazing in his own way, but Scott was something entirely different and special. He was it. He was the one I had been waiting for all this time, and I didn't regret all those lonely, empty nights. If he was my reward, he exceeded my expectations.

I dropped down on the pillow from the doggy-style position we were in, grasping for air as my whole body trembled from the orgasmic sensation I was experiencing. Scott lay on the side next to me, his hands still holding my waist. Then he traced his finger on my back while kissing my neck, and I put my face on the pillow under me, enjoying his touch.

"Are you hungry?" he asked after a few minutes, once we both came down.

"I am starving. I haven't eaten since morning back in Houston." I hadn't thought about it because all I'd been thinking about was Scott and how much I needed him. I had been starving for him, but now I needed food.

"Let me order something. I had a reservation, but we're too late now to make it."

"How late?" I asked, hoping we could still go, even though all I wanted was to sit here on this comfortable bed with my man, enjoying my beautiful life.

"One hour," he said, smiling. He knew how long we'd been here, satisfying our bodies' desires and forgetting all about eating.

We stayed on the bed talking; Scott and I couldn't stop talking. We always had something to talk about. He told me about his sisters and how excited they all were to see me. I knew it was true because Savannah had added me to their Anderson girls' group chat and introduced me to Scott's sisters. Savannah had video-called me twice already. The first time, she said she wanted to make sure I was real.

The doorbell rang. I got in the shower while Scott went to pick up our food. I went to his closet to grab one of his shirts. I loved wearing his clothes whenever I was with him, so I could feel him close to me.

I stood, shocked by what I saw. The closet was big, but there was a side full of women's clothes—like, a lot of them. I knew he had sisters, but why were their clothes in his closet? Or was there a woman living here?

"Here you are. The food is ready. Come eat," he said, holding my hand.

"Whose are those clothes for?" I asked calmly, not wanting to seem unreasonable, but I needed a reason not to freak out right then. Scott hadn't shown me any reason to doubt his love for me. I knew he loved me. I could see it in so many ways. But these clothes were driving me a little crazy.

"Those are yours. Savannah helped me pick them up so you don't have to worry when you stay here," he said.

I let out a breath I didn't know I was holding. I hated the feeling of doubt that had just crossed my mind.

"For a minute, I thought they were your ex's or something." I turned and hugged him, my towel dropping in the process.

"Listen, my love, there is no other woman in my life. Other than my sisters and mom, it's you—only you," he said, looking me right in the eyes to make his point.

"I'm sorry. I totally freaked out. Just know it would break me so much if you did that to me, and I would never forgive you," I said seriously, making sure he got my point clearly.

"You have nothing to worry about, honey."

I looked at the clothes, hung and arranged so well. Then I saw my dress, the one I'd worn in Miami. I remembered leaving it at the hotel. After the argument, I had only grabbed what I could see and left.

"You kept this?" I asked, surprised. I couldn't wear it because Scott had ruined it, but I was happy to see it.

"Yes, and this too. I couldn't leave them after the good time we had." He showed me my thong that I had been wearing with the dress.

We both laughed.

"Why didn't you give them back when you came to Houston?" I asked.

"These are my little souvenirs of you. They stay here."

I smiled. This man kept surprising me every single day.

"Let's go eat, love. The food is getting cold."

I put on his T-shirt, and we went downstairs to eat. The food was so good.

***

The next morning, I woke up to the smell of food. It was so strong, it felt like someone was cooking it on the bed. When I opened my eyes, there was a tray full of breakfast on our bed:

135

bacon, sausage, toasted bread, eggs, salad, hash browns, juice, coffee, and a cupcake.

"Wait, did you cook this?" I asked as I sat up to eat.

"I cooked some of it," he said, kissing my forehead.

The doorbell rang just as I was taking a bite of the sausage.

"Are you expecting someone?" I asked.

"No! Let me see." He walked out of the room to the door.

I sat and continued eating my delicious breakfast, which had been made by the man I loved.

"Is she here already?" I heard someone asking.

"Savannah, you can't be here. What do you want?" Scott said.

"I brought you this."

"What is this, Savannah?"

"Hi!" I said as Savannah appeared at the doorstep.

"You are really here. Wow! You are so beautiful," she said, smiling.

"Did you think she wasn't here? Come on, can you leave us alone now?" Scott said, pushing her out of the room.

"It was nice to see you, Leo," she said as they moved back to the living room.

"It was nice to see you too," I said as I heard Scott opening the door for her.

"I'm so sorry for that. Savannah can be so nosy sometimes."

"It's okay. I just hope the rest of your family likes me," I said to him. It would break my heart if they didn't.

"You are amazing. They will love you. And my mother loves anything I love. And you know I love you, so..."

I smiled, hoping he was right. I didn't have a good history with mothers-in-law.

***

After breakfast, we took a shower together, then he took me out for a quick tour. I had taken him around Houston the last time he came, so he promised to do the same. It was super cold, but we drove around in his car. We stopped and did some shopping. We had so much fun.

Now, it was time to get ready and meet the Andersons.

His parents' house was about half an hour from his condo. It was in a very rich neighborhood. The house was so big and amazing. So classic. I looked at what I was wearing, making sure I wasn't out of place. I thought I was good. I wore a long, red sweater dress with long sleeves and black boots.

I knew I looked good, and this was one of the dresses Scott had his sister buy for me.

The door opened as soon as Scott knocked on it.

"Hi! Welcome to our house," an old man, maybe in his early seventies, stood in front of us and offered me his hand.

137

"Thank you," I said, giving him my hand as we moved inside.

"Good evening, Dad," Scott said as he hugged his father.

"My name is Scott Anderson Senior. The original one." We both laughed.

"Honey, meet my father. This is Leoncia," Scott introduced me to his father as we heard a pair of heels approaching us.

"Welcome to our home, Leo. My God, you are so beautiful, and you look absolutely stunning," Hilda, Scott's mother, said.

"Thank you so much."

In a few minutes, his four sisters and Sylvia's husband came in. His sister, Sylvia, was married and pregnant with her first child.

"Come with me, let me give you a tour," Hilda said, holding my hands. I followed her; she was so nice and seemed genuinely happy to have me in her house. We went around as she showed me their amazing house. It was a truly magnificent house and incredibly beautiful. We ended up in Scott's old room, and she showed me pictures of him from his childhood.

"Wow! You have a very beautiful house and amazing children," I said as we exited Scott's old room.

"Scott mentioned you have kids. Can I see them, if it's okay with you?" she said, smiling. I wasn't sure if this was a prank. I hoped it wasn't.

"Yeah! It's okay." I opened my phone and showed her a picture of my two babies.

"Oooh! They are so beautiful. What are their names?" she asked, smiling. I still couldn't believe this was happening. Scott's mother was so nice and great in so many ways.

"Antonio and Liliana," I smiled as we reached the dining table with everyone.

"Beautiful names. I love them. At least I don't have to wait for you two to… earn grandchildren from you. You should bring them next time you come," she said, smiling.

"Let me see them. Don't let my mother scare you. She loves kids so much, I think five were not enough for her," Sylvia said as she took my phone from her mother.

Everyone admired my kids' pictures, showering them with praise for how beautiful they were. My experiences had caused me to build a wall regarding my children, but Scott's family was exceptionally kind and genuinely happy to accept me as I was.

Their housekeeper announced that the food was ready, and we all gathered at the dining table and started eating shortly after. The food was so amazing. We ate, keeping the conversations simple and exciting.

After dinner, we moved to the game room. It was a large room with various games, and we spent a considerable amount of time there before we had to leave.

Scott's mother invited us for brunch the next day. My plane was scheduled to leave at 8 PM. We would have time to go home and have sex before I left. It might take another two weeks until I saw Scott again, so whenever we were together, we used our time wisely and effectively.

We got home, had sex, and got in the shower, scrubbing each other while kissing. It felt so good to be in the arms of the man I loved, without any doubt or worries.

"Thanks, babe, for everything, my love. I still don't believe that your family really liked me. They are so beautiful inside and out," I said as Scott dried me with the towel; he always did that after we showered.

"You are beautiful inside and out. Also, you are so lovable."

"I am?" I asked, smiling.

"Yes, and I love you so much," he said, kissing me so passionately.

"I love you too, babe," I said, kissing him back.

Then we went to bed and slept. We held each other to fall asleep, and it felt amazing. I had been single for a while, and at some point, I resigned myself to the idea that I might never have a partner. But now, I wasn't sure how I had survived without this kind of intimacy, without having someone you know, without a doubt, who loves you unconditionally. I felt like with every single day that passed, I fell even deeper in love with Scott.

***

Six months passed, and they had been the best six months of my life. The long-distance relationship didn't feel the way I thought it would. Both Scott and I took time to talk every day. We knew each other's schedules and always found time to talk. We saw each other almost every other week. Sometimes I went to him, and he came to me most of the time because of the kids. I couldn't travel as freely as he could.

In March, during spring break, I took the kids to New Hampshire to visit, and Scott surprised me by buying a house, saying his condo was not kid-friendly, which was true. As expected, his family welcomed my kids so warmly, and we all had a great time. My children loved him, and he loved them back.

We traveled together on some weekends when he had business trips. Sometimes I went with him, and in the process, we bonded and had a great time together.

I had a new job, it was 100% remote, so I didn't have to go to New Hampshire only on weekends. Sometimes, I went during weekdays. I was able to visit his office, which was amazing, and we had the opportunity to connect more, even though we physically lived far apart. Also, the sex had been so great. My man was a great lover, always making sure I was satisfied beyond measure. I couldn't compare how he made me feel with anyone I had been with before him. He was one of a kind, and he was all mine.

It was July, my birthday month. I traded my car two months ago and bought a new one as an early birthday gift. However, it wasn't right to keep a car that had been bought by my ex, now that I was happily in a relationship with another man.

So, Scott was taking me on a surprise birthday vacation. I had no idea where we were going, but he just asked me to pack beach clothes, so I thought we would be around the beach. It was a four-day vacation, and I couldn't wait to start it.

I picked him up from the airport. We were leaving tomorrow.

The next day, we woke up and started driving for our trip. I realized we were heading to Galveston. I knew the road so well. I used to go to Galveston a lot when I was with Jordan. When we arrived, we went straight to the port, and I saw the large cruise ship already parked, with people boarding.

"My God, are we going on a cruise ship?" I asked, surprised. Two months ago, we had been talking about places and things we would like to do. I remembered telling him I would love to go on a cruise ship because I had never been before, and now here we were, ready to fulfill one of my dreams.

"Yes, love, we are."

I kissed him so hard; he was the best of all the best things in my life.

"I love you so much, my love," I said, kissing him more.

"I love you, darling," he said, kissing me back.

We boarded the ship and went straight to our room. The first thing we did as the ship started moving was make love. I had wanted to make love on a ship so badly, and the bed was right by a small window. We could see the sea as we passionately made love.

Four days flew by so fast. We passed so many places. I remembered Costa Maya, Mexico, Honduras, Montego Bay, and other places. We had a great time exploring all the places. We only slept a few hours; we were always moving around, kissing, or having sex. So many times, we even had sex in the restrooms. We just wanted to know how it would feel, and we were certainly not disappointed.

We had so much fun. On the last night, Scott reserved a dinner date for us at one of the restaurants inside the ship. It was so thoughtful and amazing. That was how Scott was; always thinking of ways to make me happy. I was so grateful that I had found him, that he was mine, and we were doing this life together.

We got to the restaurant, and there weren't many people. The restaurant was at the top of the ship. We could see the sea. They seated us at a table that was somewhat isolated from the others, and I liked the feeling. I was at peace and so happy.

I had loved and been loved before, but this was so different. The love I felt for Scott was so free and genuine. I had no doubt in myself or him. You could call me blind, but I was sure that with Scott by my side, I had nothing to worry about. I never thought that happiness like this could exist. I could see how he felt too, and it matched me completely. Like magnets, we pulled each other closer and tighter in all possible ways. I could swear that sometimes we thought alike. I would call to tell him something, and he would be calling me about the same thing.

I looked at him, thinking about how happy he made me. All we needed now was to get married. I wasn't sure what he was waiting for to pop the question, but I was going to propose to him if he didn't do it.

We finished our dinner. It was amazing. I loved everything. As usual, he picked my food, and I picked his. We always did that when we went out. There was a man with a guitar who started singing next to us. The song was *All of Me* by John Legend, which was my favorite.

Scott stood, offering me his hand, and we started slow dancing.

"Thank you, my love, for the most amazing birthday," I said, kissing him on the lips. I wiped lipstick off, then let him go as the waitress said something behind us.

"This is for you, ma'am," she said, handing me a fake red heart on a flower branch. Attached to it were small words written: "OPEN ME."

I twisted the side and opened it. A ring! There was an engagement ring inside, a silver one with a Tanzanite stone at its center. Tanzanite is from my mother's country, Tanzania. The fact that he found that and included it in this ring made it so special and unique.

I turned around, and I didn't see Scott for a second. Then I realized he was on one knee in front of me.

"Oooh! My God," I said, covering my face, not believing this was really happening. Scott took the flower and pulled out the ring, then he said the words that melted my heart completely. If I had any doubts, which I didn't, this would have been the moment to forget anything that might hinder my union with him.

"Leoncia, my love. First, I need you to know that I have never loved any woman before the way I love you. You are my sunshine, my peace, my future, my forever, and it would be a great honor if you said yes to being my wife. So, Leoncia, would you please be my wife?"

"Yes, yes, yes. I will be your wife, love. I will marry you now if it's possible," I said, pulling him up for a hug.

We were both crying from happiness. I couldn't believe I was engaged to the most handsome man alive.

"She said yes!" he said louder. "I love you, darling," Scott said while kissing me, and I kissed him back.

"I love you."

People around us were clapping, and I realized the waitress had been taking pictures and videos. I was so happy and grateful for everything. Now, my life felt completely perfect.

We went back to our room, and the second we got there, we didn't waste a minute. We made love so passionately. I felt incredible to be in Scott's arms as he hovered on top of me, thrusting in and out of me while kissing every single part of me passionately. He was everything I wanted and needed and more. I knew at that moment I was the luckiest woman alive.

We arrived at my place the next day around five p.m. All I wanted was to stay home, call my mother, tell her the good news—the best news, actually—and have more alone time with Scott. On the other hand, Scott wanted us to go for dinner and celebrate. I knew he was right—it's not every day I get engaged. So we got ready quickly and headed to the restaurant. We needed to be there by six-thirty.

I wore a white dress that hugged my body well. I had a really nice body; I was never going to complain about that again. I knew, other than my personality, my physical body drove Scott madly in love with me, and I loved the way he cherished every single part of it.

My phone rang as we entered the restaurant. It was my mother, so I picked it up as Scott talked to the receptionist about our table.

"Hello!"

"Are you guys back already?"

"Yes, we are back, Mama."

"Good, you are coming for dinner, right?" she asked.

"No! We are eating dinner at a restaurant, celebrating."

"Celebrating what?"

Scott called me through the glass door as I saw the waiter ready to take us to our table.

"Mama, I have to go. I will call you later."

I got in and followed them as Scott took my hand and intertwined our fingers.

"Congratulations."

I moved my head up as we entered this room full of people saying, "Congratulations." In a few seconds, I realized it was every person we knew—friends and family. Both my grandparents were there—my mother's mother and my father's parents. My mother, aunties, uncles, my friends, Scott's family—yes, his whole family—his friends, even some from

Miami, were there. I saw Linda, the girl who kept me company at the party in Miami.

"I knew you guys would get married soon after that day," Linda said, hugging me. "Congratulations. If he didn't pop the question, I would have popped it for him," she added, and we both laughed.

Linda grew up as a neighbor to the Andersons but left New Hampshire after she got a job in New York. I had met her a couple of times already because Savannah, Scott, and Linda were best friends. At first, I thought I should worry about her, but I found out nothing ever happened between them, and they weren't attracted to each other at all.

"Did you know about this? How did they know we got engaged?" I asked Scott, wondering.

"Your mother and Savannah organized everything; I told them I was going to propose," he said.

"And I was sure my daughter was going to say yes. That's why we came up with the plan," my mother said as she hugged me.

"Yeah! Your mother was so sure you would say yes. I was terrified. I am so glad you said yes. She said yes, everyone!" Scott yelled the last part, and everyone cheered and clapped.

My mother took me aside and hugged me.

"Are you happy?" she asked.

"Very happy," I said, smiling, looking around; all the important people in my life were here.

"He is so thoughtful. You should know he went to Detroit and visited your father's grave, asking for your hand in marriage," my mother said, and a tear came down her left eye. "I am so sorry for my participation in your last marriage. I know this is different, but I want you to be happy and know it's okay if this is not what you want," she said, holding my cheeks, which were also full of tears now.

"I have never wanted anything this way. I love him, and he is the one I was waiting for all this time, Mama."

"I am so happy for you, my love."

She hugged me one more time, then joined our family. Everyone came to congratulate Scott and me.

Someone opened the door, and I was surprised to see Juliana, Jordan's sister, getting in. She and I were still friends, but we were not that close since I broke up with her brother, and she moved to New York.

"Juliana, what are you doing here?" I asked, surprised as she hugged me.

"Well, I was in town and I decided to visit Liliana. You know she is my favorite, and I found your mother preparing for this. I had to come and congratulate you, my dear. I am so happy for you," she said, smiling.

"Really? I thought you wouldn't be happy for obvious reasons," I said, not wanting to talk about it…not at my engagement party anyway.

"Leo, you are a nice person. Whatever happened already happened. I love you, and I wish you a lot of happiness."

I hugged her, then Savannah announced that the food was ready, and we all started getting our food. I made sure the kids got their food. When I came back for mine, I found Scott had already picked it for me. He was always one step ahead, making my life easier and better.

"Thank you, babe." I kissed him, and we started eating.

Juliana left right after she finished her food. I didn't ask her not to tell Jordan because I knew he would hear about it anyway. We had so many common friends.

After dinner, everybody started leaving. We stayed until the last person left, then went back home. My mother left with the kids, and we went home alone. Scott's family was staying in a hotel and would be leaving the next day. It was wonderful for them to come and support us as we celebrated our engagement.

I sat on the bed after taking off my makeup and having a quick shower. Scott was sitting on the loveseat in my room, answering some emails. He had been out of work for some time. I could imagine how behind he must have been, and he was trying to catch up.

My phone rang, and it was an unsaved number. I usually never picked up numbers I didn't know, but I wondered who was calling me this late. It was almost eleven p.m. I picked it up.

"Hallow!"

"Hi! Sweetheart."

It was him. Jordan. I would know his voice anywhere. I used to get turned on by his voice, but now that Scott was right across from me, all I felt was panic. How do you explain to your soon-to-be husband a call from an ex at this hour? The last thing I needed was to give Scott any type of reason to doubt me. Trust had been our strongest foundation from the day he came to my house and I became his, and he became mine.

"Jordan!" I breathed his name quietly, hoping Scott didn't hear me. He moved his eyes from the laptop to me. I knew he was wondering who was calling. I usually didn't receive calls at night, especially if he was around. I mostly talked to my mother, and when Scott was here, she knew not to disturb us.

"Listen, I know it's late and I apologize for calling, but please don't hang up," he said quickly.

"What do you want?" I asked, turning the other side so I wouldn't alarm Scott. I debated getting out of the room or running to the bathroom, but it would raise suspicion if I did that. I knew I didn't have anything to hide.

"I was told you are engaged, and I need to hear from you if it's true," he said, and I couldn't figure out if he was angry or disappointed.

"Yes, I am," I answered confidently.

"So, does that mean your kids are not a priority anymore, or was it just for me?" he said, reminding me of what I said to him a few years ago. "This clearly confirms that you never loved me. At least not the way I did," he said calmly.

"That's not true," I said, hoping he understood without me going into details.

Scott closed his laptop and moved to the other side of the bed.

"I know maybe you hate me for that, but I hope you find what I have found one day."

"Leoncia, you are the greatest love of my life. I would never hate you. Also, I doubt there is anyone like you out here."

"I really need to go, thanks for calling," I said, trying to end the conversation.

"Wait, Cia. Are you happy?" he asked me. It was the same question my mother had asked a few hours ago, and for some reason, it made me smile again, thinking about how happy I was.

"I am."

"Then congratulations. I hope he treats you right because you deserve the world," he said, and I cut the phone after saying a soft, "Thank you."

I jumped on top of Scott, who was lying on the bed with his back on the mattress. I was wearing Scott's shirt, and he was only in boxers. I started kissing his little nipples, already in need of him.

"Who was that on the phone?" Scott asked, unbothered by what I was busy doing.

"My ex, Jordan," I said, turning to look at him, hoping he wasn't angry at me.

"Why did he call you at this time, and why did you pick up his call?" he asked, sounding annoyed. We both sat on the bed now.

"I didn't know it was him. I didn't have his number, and he just wanted to congratulate me," I said, trying to calm him down, my hands on his chest, playing it off like the call wasn't important, which it somehow was. I found out that Jordan didn't hate me.

"Why did you keep talking to him, knowing it's him?" he asked as I started kissing his neck.

"Babe! First, you have nothing to worry about," I said, holding his face as I jumped on top of his thighs.

"And I needed this. I never talked to him after the day I broke up with him. This call helped me clear things with him. I really thought he hated me," I said, trying to reduce the tension as I massaged his head slowly with my nails.

"Why did you two break up?" he asked. I never told anyone why we broke up…mostly because I didn't regret it, and I would do it again for my kids in a heartbeat.

"We dated during the time Liliana's asthma was bad and his career was rising. So I had to choose between them, and I chose my kid," I said, smiling.

"Did you love him?" he asked seriously. I saw he was trying to figure out if I still had feelings for Jordan.

"Listen, babe, he is one of the important people in my past, and yes, I loved him. But now, in this very moment, you are the one I am in love with. My sexy fiancé. Given that, can we stop talking about the past and can you make love to your horny wife-to-be instead?" I said and kissed him like my life depended on it.

Scott held the shirt I was wearing from the top and tore it apart, turning me on even more. He did that a lot when he couldn't wait or was on a mission to get right to the point. It gave the sense of him claiming me on a manly level. It was super sexy and did things to my body.

He turned me around, laying me down on my back. Then he came on top of me, not wanting to waste any time. Neither did I. I spread my legs apart, ready for him, and when he slid into me, I closed my eyes, feeling him whole. I still couldn't believe I would have him like this for the rest of my life. I wasn't sure how I got this lucky.

A few minutes later, he turned me around. I lay on my stomach, and he pulled my right leg up to my hips and left the other straight down. Then he entered my vagina from behind, holding my butt with one free hand. While thrusting in and out, he was on his knees on the bed, bending over me. This was our favorite position, and we always did it. I always reached climax in just a few minutes, and he always made sure I had multiple orgasms.

"Ohh! My God, Ooh! My God, Yes, Yes, Yes. Mmmmmh!" I screamed as I orgasmed for the third time, and Scott got there with me, exploding inside me like a volcano.

After that, we stayed on the bed, kissing until we fell asleep, our bodies fully satisfied.

The next day, we all met at my mother's house. She prepared brunch and invited Scott's family too. They all left after that.

***

Two months passed since Scott and I got engaged. We had already picked a date in February next year for our wedding. Scott was moving to Houston. His company had opened a new branch office there, and he would be managing it.

We discussed where we would live after getting married, as we were both not ready to continue the long-distance arrangement. One of us had to move.

Scott decided he would be the one moving because the kids were in school, and he would be spending more time in Houston anyway with the new investment his company acquired.

His mother wasn't thrilled, but she was so kind-hearted and happy for us. She said as long as her son was happy, she was okay with the distance. Scott hadn't left his hometown since college, when he lived in New York for four years, so I could imagine how his family felt. We promised to visit at least once a month. I knew Scott would be going back and forth because of work. He started taking some of his meetings virtually, which made the amount of time he was gone significantly less.

We had been looking for a house since he came to Houston. My lease ending in March, so I already knew I wasn't renewing it.

We were having the wedding in New Hampshire on February . We already got the hall, and Scott's family was going to take care of everything.

I appreciated that they allowed me to handle the dress and all aspects of my makeup and hair. I already had a makeup artist who would be with me the whole time to make sure my makeup was on point.

I still needed to find a dress. I knew I had time, but it stressed me out. None of the dresses I found felt right. Making me think I would have to custom make one.

Chapter XI:
Now, Always and Forever

I was on my way home from the store when I decided to pick up the mail from the mailbox. I parked in the garage and checked the mail so I could discard the ones I didn't need in the trash can there.

To my surprise, I saw a letter summoning me to a child custody hearing filed by Pablo.

"What is this?" I read it quickly, then grabbed my phone and called Pablo immediately.

"Hallo! Bride-to-be," he said when he picked up.

"What the fuck, Pablo? You really want to fight for my kids' custody?"

"Cia, they are my kids too. Did you think I'd let my kids be raised by that white man of yours?" he said.

"So this is about race? Aren't you married to a white woman?" I asked, getting so angry at him.

"It's not about race. I just won't allow any other man to raise my kids. It's time I take them so you can keep your liberation and spread those legs of yours freely."

I couldn't believe him. This was a man I had wanted to be with forever? This maniac?

"So, you wanted me to remain single, taking care of these kids alone for the rest of my life? Are you fucking kidding me?" I couldn't stop my voice from shaking with rage.

"I don't care what you do with your life, Cia. Just know I'm going to take my kids and keep them safe from your immoral behavior," he said.

"What are you talking about?" I asked in shock. I never thought this day would ever arrive.

"I have our divorce agreement that shows you were the one responsible for our marriage not working. We wouldn't be here if you hadn't slept with my best friend," he said. I could feel the anger in his voice.

"Are you sick in the head? Both you and I know that you did the same thing. And multiple times. So don't play games with me."

"Well, the game is on. I'm taking my kids, Cia."

He hung up after that. I called him again, but he didn't pick up.

I was so angry. I couldn't believe him. Whether he was crazy or delusional, no one was taking my babies, not unless it was over my dead body.

I went inside. Scott was still cooking. I had left earlier to find one of the ingredients we didn't have that he needed for the dish he was preparing. The kids were running around and playing games as I entered the kitchen.

"Did you get it?" Scott asked as he felt me come close. He turned around and saw that I was crying.

"Darling, what's wrong?" he asked, hugging me after switching off the stove.

I cried in his arms for a few minutes, trying to regain my strength. He kept comforting me as I wept, caressing my hair and rubbing my back.

"What happened?" he asked again as we sat at the dining table. He was holding my waist with one hand, the other on my left cheek. I loved how he cared and attentively ensured my well-being. I smiled and then handed him the letter I had received.

He opened it and read the documents, his face stone cold. "He wants custody of them?" he asked, surprised.

"Yes. He's claiming I'm not a good mother because I cheated on him. He discussed the divorce agreement, which he cited as the reason for our separation. I don't even know where that divorce paper is. All I know is I can't let him take my kids," I said, crying.

"He won't. Listen, we are going to hire the best lawyer in Texas—or America, for that matter. He'll never take them," he said, wiping away my tears.

"Listen, he has no grounds to take them. I'm not a lawyer, but I know being a bad partner doesn't make someone a bad parent," he added.

"I can't lose my kids. I won't survive without them, Scott," I said, crying even more.

"My love, he's not going to take them. I'll make sure of that. Don't worry. Let me call my lawyer and ask him to find us the best lawyer for you. It will be alright."

He hugged me for a few seconds, then took his phone and called his lawyer while continuing to cook.

By the time we were eating, he had already received the phone number of the lawyer who would represent me, and we had set an appointment for the next day to meet and discuss the matter.

I was relieved after we met with the lawyer and reviewed my options. I had a strong case, considering I had been the sole caregiver for the kids since day one. My criminal record was clean; there was no reason to declare me unfit to be their mother. The fact that I was engaged to be married also eliminated and discredited Pablo's claims that I was a cheater who moved from one man to another.

From that point on, I wasn't supposed to contact Pablo, and if he called, I wasn't supposed to answer. My lawyer would be the one to communicate with him and his lawyer going forward.

Two months passed. The custody case had already started. I was able to retrieve some photos of text messages and phone calls I had taken from Pablo's phone back when we were married, and I suspected he was cheating on me. So when his lawyer tried to paint me as a bad mother who kept moving from one man to another, not providing a stable environment for my kids, my lawyer brought that evidence to show that Pablo had also been moving from one woman to another. The judge dismissed infidelity as a valid reason to question either of us as parents.

My lawyer also presented financial evidence showing that I had raised the kids myself without Pablo's help all these years. He even showed the credit card that was supposed to be paid by both of us, highlighting that I had ended up paying it alone. He submitted birthday pictures where Pablo was absent, hospital bills, and my insurance, which included the kids. Pablo was in the military but hadn't added his kids to his insurance and couldn't explain why he hadn't been in their lives as he was supposed to.

Last week, Pablo's mother had called my mother asking if she could see the kids. I told my mother to tell her to come today. It was the weekend, and I was home. I also needed to talk to her and put a stop to the narrative that I was keeping the kids from them. They weren't the kind of people I wanted around my children, but I couldn't ignore the fact that they were still family. I did a lot of things for my kids, and if tolerating Pablo's family would give my children the best possible childhood experience, then that's what I would do. The last thing I wanted was for my kids to grow up thinking the reason their father and his family weren't around was because of my selfishness.

Mrs. Martin came about half an hour ago. Scott was in New Hampshire, so it was just me and the kids. She played with them while I made dinner.

"Can we talk?" she said, approaching the kitchen.

"About what?" I asked. I had no desire to talk about her son at all.

"Why don't you drop the charges and talk about an agreement?"

I switched off the stove. I couldn't believe she thought I was the one who had filed for full custody. Of course, she would think that. This woman always believed I was the bad one when it came to her son. She believed him blindly. I knew she hadn't come to court, but I wasn't about to let her keep blaming me for everything that happened between me and Pablo.

"Your own son is the one who can drop the charges," I said, looking her straight in the eyes.

"What do you mean? He said you filed for child support."

"He's the one who took me to court. He said it was 'game on.' I'm going to show him that my kids are not going to be part of his crazy games," I said angrily. She looked surprised, as usual; she always believed whatever her son told her.

"That's not true," she said, looking at me, tears in her eyes.

"You know what's not true? That I was the one who broke our marriage," I said, making sure she heard and understood me.

"I was nineteen and pregnant when my husband, the father of my kids, told me he never loved me. Then he admitted to cheating on me with other women. I agree, my decision to sleep with his friend wasn't great, but at the time, it was the only way I could feel alive and loved."

I turned around, took my bottle of water from the kitchen counter, and drank.

"I'm so sorry for what he did," she said.

I smiled. "You should apologize for yourself too. I called you and talked to you about what he was doing several times, but I guess you never believed me. I hope you're different with his current wife. I just want you to know your son is the worst human being I've ever met. And this lawsuit he filed proves that he will never change. So now go home to him and ask him to drop it. But be sure of one thing: I am not going to stop fighting if he ever plays games with my kids' lives."

Mrs. Martin picked up her bag from the couch, then said, "I'm sorry for everything," as she opened the door.

"You're a mother like me, so I hope you understand that I will fight to the death for my children. Nothing will stop me from keeping them with me," I said, making sure she got my point clearly. She walked out and left.

A week later, the judge gave the ruling. He granted me full custody and the right to keep the kids with me. Pablo was allowed to be part of their lives as long as he communicated with me before taking them. They could stay with him for no more than a month, and I had to be informed of their whereabouts at all times.

He was also ordered to pay me back for half of all the expenses I had incurred raising the kids alone, including the debts he had left me with. From now on, he would pay 50% of everything the kids needed for school and home.

Although I didn't need anything from him, I would take the money and save it for their college fund, something I had started when I had Liliana.

We walked out of the courtroom after the ruling. Outside, our lawyer told us how good the outcome was for me. Then Pablo walked up and stood next to Scott.

"She's a cheater. Keep your friends away from her," he said, looking up at Scott. Scott was a couple of inches taller than him.

"Does your wife keep your aunties away from you?" Scott said, smiling while Pablo grew angry, knowing his warning had done nothing to faze Scott.

"And you should know that I love Leoncia," Scott added, "and that the past—especially the one including you—is just the past. It has no importance in our life."

He held me by the waist, pulling me closer to him, claiming me as his—something I already was.

"I see you're long gone. I'll pray she doesn't ruin your life," Pablo said.

That made me snap.

"What's hard to believe, Pablo? That I won the case, or the fact that I'm way better than the nineteen-year-old you told would never be loved?"

He looked at me and stepped slightly back as I moved in front of him, wanting him to get my point. Maybe then he would realize how much better off I was without him.

"I know it hurts you to see me like this. Listen, I don't care how selfish you want to be, but let me assure you, next time you play this little stupid game with my kids, I will not be this nice," I said, glaring at him.

"I hope you'll do right by your kids now. But don't worry, I'm already more of a father to them than you'll ever be," Scott added, and it was true. My kids knew and liked him more than their own father.

"I am their father," Pablo said. I could see he was completely defeated, and I liked it.

"Unfortunately, you are. But fortunately, they'll have a bonus father in their lives who will love them unconditionally. And he isn't selfish like you," I said, then held Scott's hand as we exited the building. I didn't want to spend another second in Pablo's presence.

When we got home, my mother and Savannah were there. They surprised us with an early dinner celebration to mark my win in the case. It was about time Pablo started taking care of his kids, just a little. I was never going to ask him to do anything, but I was glad he did what he did. Maybe now he'd finally step up. My kids deserved better.

We already had the house we were going to move into next month, and I was so excited. I woke up early that day because I had a doctor's appointment. I wasn't working at the moment, as my contract job had ended two weeks ago, and Scott and I had decided that, with the wedding approaching, I would find a new job after our honeymoon.

So I spent my time decorating our house, packing, planning the wedding, and being a good wife-to-be to my man.

"Where are you going this early?" Scott asked as I finished putting on my shoes.

"Sorry, did I wake you up?" I said, kissing his forehead.

"It's okay! So where are you going?" he asked again.

"I have a gynecologist appointment. I need them to replace my IUD," I said, picking up my purse.

"What do you mean, replacing it?" he asked, moving to a sitting position.

"They're going to put another one," I said, knowing he understood me clearly the first time.

"So you don't want to get pregnant?" he asked, surprised.

"Not right now," I said.

"How long have you planned not to have kids with me?" he asked. I could hear the disappointment and sadness in his voice.

"No, baby, I want to have kids with you. But we've got a lot going on right now," I said, hoping he understood.

"The move and the wedding will be done within two to three months. After that, what will stop us from having a baby?" he asked. I could see he was hurt. I never wanted him to feel like I didn't want to have a baby with him. We just never talked about it.

"Babe, I want to have kids with you, and we'll talk about it when I come back. But I need to leave now before I'm late for my appointment." I kissed him on the cheek and lips. "I love you."

"I love you," he said, kissing me back. Then I left and went to the hospital.

My mother had taken the kids the day before. She always did that to give me and Scott time alone, and I was so grateful for it.

After my appointment, I went to the store and bought some red lace lingerie. I had a couple of them at home, and I knew Scott loved it when I wore them. He had already gone to work, so it was just me at home.

When Scott came home, he was surprised by what I had prepared for him. I turned off the main lights and used soft lighting and candles. I cooked his favorite meal. The bedroom was also filled with candles and flowers, making it look romantic.

"Wow! Are we celebrating something? I didn't forget our anniversary, right? I know it's not our birthdays," he said as he entered the bedroom.

"We're celebrating having a baby," I said, smiling. I had decided not to put in a new IUD. I was ready to get pregnant.

"Are you pregnant?" he asked seriously.

"No. But we can officially start trying to have one," I said, kissing him. I still had a robe on, so he hadn't seen what I was wearing.

"I love that. What happened to 'we'll talk later'?" he asked, smiling.

"We're talking. But can you use fewer words and more action?"

He pulled me close and kissed me passionately. He opened my robe and saw the lingerie.

"You really want to get pregnant today," he said, smiling. I laughed so hard.

Within minutes, he ripped the lingerie in the middle, as usual, turning me on even more. I lay on the bed as he devoured me, driving me crazy in the process. I loved this man so much. He was everything I had ever asked for and more.

My life has changed and elevated so much since I met Scott. He made me happy and made me feel loved beyond my wildest imagination. Scott was my person, the kind of person I would jump off a cliff for if he asked me to.

We made love, then ate, then got into it again and again. As we lay in each other's arms, I believed I was the luckiest woman alive. I didn't know what the future held, but I knew I would always love Scott.

It was my wedding day. Everything was perfect, exactly how Scott and I wanted it. The ceremony was in New Hampshire. My auntie was my maid of honor, and Scott's sisters were my bridesmaids. They had both been so happy when I asked them.

My babies were the little ring bearer and flower girl. They were excited and so happy.

Scott and I both cried as I walked down the aisle, which was decorated beautifully. I still couldn't believe I was getting married with an actual wedding ceremony, and I was so happy.

We said our vows in front of our family.

Scott's Vows

"Leoncia, I never believed in falling in love before you. I always thought it was not possible to love someone the way I love you. You make me so happy, and I promise you today that I will always try to be the best for you, because since I met you, I've become the best version of myself. I love you so much, my love, now and forever."

Leoncia's Vows

"I had given up on love when I met you; I came to realize I never knew what true love really was. Thank you for showing me this amazing kind of love that is free, secure, unconditional, true, and genuine. Thank you for loving my kids as your own from day one. I was raised as an only child; sharing was never in my vocabulary. However, with you and your strong, loving family, I learned how to share you with the rest of your family positively. You brought back the peace in my life that I never thought I had lost along the way. I love you so much more for choosing to love me as I am. I will love you always and forever, my love."

Chapter X:
Five Years Later

Well, where should I start? It has been five amazing years of my life so far, and I am hoping for many more.

Unfortunately, we lost Scott Senior, my husband's father, three years ago. We moved to New Hampshire after that, and Scott became the president and CEO of their family company, Anderson Real Estate.

My mother married her boyfriend, and they had been traveling the world since we left Texas. Savannah and Vanessa also got married, three and two years ago, respectively.

Jordan got married two years ago. He invited me to the wedding, but I didn't go. I had a little kid, but also, after I saw the woman he was marrying (she looked a lot like me), I knew it would be awkward for me to be at the ceremony.

Pablo was stationed in Europe with his family for three years. They returned six months ago, and he is now living in Chicago. He had learned his lesson after the case and had been behaving, staying in his lane respectfully.

I had two more children with Scott: Samantha, who is four years old, and Louise, who is two years old. I am seven months pregnant and am having a baby boy. Today is the baby shower, and it is being held at our house.

Yes, we bought a house after moving here. It's huge; three stories with numerous rooms, ideal for our family. Each kid has their own room, and we still have more for guests, even if we add another baby. I honestly don't know if I'm done having babies. I love how big my family is; it's so different from how I grew up. I've always loved and hoped to have a big family myself.

I hired a party planner to help me, and I was delighted with what she did with my backyard. Everything is white and blue. I'm wearing a short, tight blue dress that hugs my body so well. I always look good when I'm pregnant. I'm so lucky none of my pregnancies have ever been difficult. I'm the type of woman who could make you think childbirth is simple and easy.

My gender reveal for this baby boy was amazing too. I had friends and family over for lunch, and we had all my kids line up with white cotton candy that has blue inside. By the time they finish, their mouths turn blue. I was so happy, but not as happy as Scott.

I'm sitting on a decorated couch in front of everyone. I have so many friends now. My mother-in-law and her daughters added me to a social group of women here, mothers and wives in the community. It helps me learn different things, and I have a couple of friends here today who are all celebrating with me and my family.

We haven't started the party yet because I'm waiting for my mother. She was supposed to arrive yesterday, but her flight got canceled due to bad weather. Fortunately, she's finally landed, and the driver is bringing her over.

Just as we begin the celebration, my mother walks in. "I hope I'm not late for my beautiful little Scott's baby shower!"

she exclaims, drawing everyone's attention. I immediately realized that she wasn't supposed to reveal the baby's name out loud.

"Mama!" I say, a little shocked as I look at her. It takes her a moment, but then she realizes her mistake. "My God, I'm so sorry!" she says, turning to Scott, who has just arrived.

We had intended to keep the baby's name a surprise until the birth, but I had told my mother the name before she left, wanting her to feel included in our secret. I guess I should have been more cautious.

"You're calling him Scott?" Mrs. Anderson, Scott's mother, asks in surprise.

"Yes, Mom. He's going to be Scott Anderson the Second," Scott replies with a smile as he hugs me.

His mother steps in to embrace both of us. "Thank you so much for this. Your father would have been so happy, my love," she says, lovingly holding Scott's face with one hand and mine with the other.

The party goes on as everyone congratulates us and joins in celebrating the joy of having another child.

As I celebrate the arrival of my fifth child, I have so much to be grateful for in my life. I know it hasn't been easy to get to where I am, but I wouldn't change anything. Life presents us with many situations that can break us just as much as they make us strong. As I reflect on my past and all the challenges I've faced, I know I'm exactly where I'm meant to be.

I'm grateful and blessed to share my life with the love of my life and our wonderful children.

THE END.